# The Outside World

By Lucy Ellen Bender
Illustrated by Ivan Moon

RESOURCE *Publications* • Eugene, Oregon

Resource Publications
A division of Wipf and Stock Publishers
199 W 8th Ave, Suite 3
Eugene, OR 97401

The Outside World
By Bender, Lucy Ellen
Copyright©1969 by Bender, Lucy Ellen
ISBN 13: 978-1-5326-7012-1
Publication date 9/18/2018
Previously published by Herald Press, 1969

# Contents

# 1

# One Among Many

Ruth Ann Miller felt her heart beat faster against her starched, hand-me-down dress. The yellow bus rolled down the hill, and at last she saw the high school in the valley—the consolidated school with nearly a thousand students. Each time she had passed the school last summer Ruth Ann's fear of the school's bigness had grown. What would it be like—her first day at this strange school?

She could have attended the small Christian day school, but Mamma had been sick. With all the doctor bills, Daddy couldn't afford to pay the tuition there any longer.

Ruth Ann reached up to push her dark hair into place. She hoped her braids would stay neat under her covering all day. She hadn't even dreamed of asking her mother whether she should wear her prayer covering to this school. At Christian day school, everyone wore it. But when she got on the bus, Ruth Ann felt the curious stares of the other students.

*Oh, I hope no one asks about my covering. I'll bet they'll make fun of me,* she thought, wishing Mary, her friend from church, were with her. Mary would have worn her covering, too. Then Ruth Ann wouldn't have felt so alone.

The bus drove up to the school. Ruth Ann got up, carrying her lunch box and her tablet and pencil. These had been standard equipment at the other school, but now she tried to hide them in the folds of her skirt, for no one else was carrying a lunch, and most of the students had notebooks under their arms. Ruth Ann had never felt so out of place.

Getting off the bus, a boy jostled her and her lunch box crashed to the sidewalk. Her sandwiches flew across the grass, and the jar containing peaches broke into a million tiny pieces. Ruth Ann's dark eyes gleamed with anger as she bent to pick up her sandwiches.

"Dumb Dutchman," she heard a boy mumble as he went past her. Ruth Ann felt like flinging her lunch box at him. She glared at the boy. He certainly wasn't like Brian, one of her friends at church. Brian would never intentionally hurt someone's feelings.

She wished herself back in the little country school she'd loved so dearly. There no unfriendly eyes stared at her and her simple way of dressing. At the moment she hated the new school, and she knew she couldn't like anything in it. She was too different from everyone else. She could see herself starting off to school every day, alone and always eternally different.

In homeroom she sat in the farthest corner. The

6

teacher had not come in and Ruth Ann noticed several girls nearby talking in a low tone. She felt they might be talking about her and wished she had stayed home.

As Ruth Ann brooded, one of the girls came toward her. She noticed the girl's brown hair swinging cleanly about her shoulders. Her well-cut jumper would never have been a hand-me-down from a cousin.

"You're new, aren't you?" the girl said.

"Yes, I am." Ruth Ann wondered whether the girl would ask next why she was wearing that "funny little hat."

"My name is Roxy Davidson," the girl went on. "I'll try to show you around today. Maybe some of our classes will be the same."

Ruth Ann opened her eyes wide at this first expression of kindness in the new school. "That's very nice of you," she smiled gratefully.

Then one of the girls aimed a question at her. "Do you think you'll be going to the school dances?"

Ruth Ann stiffened. "No, I don't think so," she murmured. She felt Roxy's eyes on her.

As they walked to their first class, Roxy put a friendly hand on her shoulder. "Don't feel bad about not dancing, Ruth Ann. Gretchen didn't mean any harm. She just didn't know."

"Why, how did you know?" Ruth Ann gasped.

"Well, you're a Mennonite, aren't you? We have some Mennonite neighbors and they never attend dances. I just added two and two."

Ruth Ann thought Roxy's smile was the friendliest she'd ever seen.

7

She relaxed as English class began. English had always been her best subject. Mrs. Jensen announced, "Since it is the first day of school, we will just write a short composition on *Coming Back to School*. Make it no more than one hundred words."

Ruth Ann scratched hastily in her tablet. Compositions were her strong point.

After she'd finished she sat staring out the window. School might be bearable after all. She seemed to have one friend—Roxy. She could make more friends.

Ruth Ann almost jumped as Mrs. Jensen stopped beside her desk. "Are you finished?" Ruth Ann watched Mrs. Jensen's mouth as she shaped each word carefully.

"Yes, I am," she answered, wondering whether Mrs. Jensen always spoke so precisely.

"May I see what you have done?"

Ruth Ann handed her paper to Mrs. Jensen and watched her thin angular body march to the front of the room.

*Goodness, she's going to read my paper out loud,* Ruth Ann thought in panic. She wanted to run and snatch the paper from the teacher's hand. *What would the class think when they heard her composition?*

Mrs. Jensen read. "Going to school is different now. Now I'm one of many. Before I was one of few. Here in this sea of faces no one really counts for much.

"Can it really matter that I am so different? Does it really matter that my hair is fastened in braids under a prayer covering, my clothes are hand-me-downs, and that I carry my lunch in a box?

8

"No, it shouldn't matter, for I am only one among so many." Mrs. Jensen's clipped voice ceased, and Ruth Ann could almost hear the silence.

Even with her eyes closed in embarrassment, Ruth Ann felt the pressure of Roxy's hand on hers and heard her whisper, "You're very nice, different or not."

Mrs. Jensen broke the stillness. "You really write very well, Ruth Ann. Do you see, boys and girls, what she has done with very simple words? Also notice that she has written about her own experience. Always write about something that you know. By the way, Ruth Ann, you're a Mennonite, aren't you?"

Ruth Ann came quickly alert with apprehension "Yes" she almost whispered.

"I've often wondered about those prayer coverings you wear." Mrs. Jensen smiled. "Could you tell us a little bit about that practice? I'm sure we would be interested in knowing."

Ruth Ann cringed. This was the moment she had dreaded. Her mouth went dry with uncertainty.

"Well," Ruth Ann began slowly. She heard someone titter behind her. Turning, she saw a girl with little gimlet eyes grinning unpleasantly at her.

"I'm sorry," Mrs. Jensen said. "I didn't mean to embarrass you. I was only curious."

Ruth Ann plunged into determined speech. If her teacher wanted to know about the covering, she would tell her, "We call these little veils prayer coverings. In the Bible the Apostle Paul instructs women to be veiled when praying. Since we are instructed to pray without ceasing too, some of us believe in wearing a veil all the time." Ruth Ann

10

caught her breath with a painful gasp.

The room was silent. Surely now someone would laugh. The girl of the gimlet eyes did not disappoint her. Her laughter broke the silence. Then Ruth Ann heard Roxy whisper to the unpleasant girl "Louella, why don't you keep still?"

Ruth Ann's clenched hands relaxed. Now she felt sure she had one friend, but she wished she could go back to her school where everyone was her friend.

At home that evening she went to the piano and thundered into a wild piece of music. Daddy heard her playing and came to the door. "What's wrong now?" he asked. He knew that Ruth Ann always played intensely when she was upset.

"I hate that school," she blurted. "I never want to go back again. Why can't I go back to Christian day school?" Then she stopped, seeing the hurt in Daddy's eyes. "I'm sorry. I know you can't help it, Daddy. I'll be all right."

She ran upstairs and began a letter to her cousin Beth, an Amish girl who lived in the South. *You're lucky your parents didn't let you finish high school in the public school,* she wrote. Cousin Beth had wanted desperately to complete her high school education, but had to stay at home and work after she reached her sixteenth birthday. *I envy you,* Ruth Ann went on. *You have no idea how awful it is with all those curious eyes staring at you. I hate it already.*

That evening when she went to bed. Ruth Ann thought sadly of the next days. *I'll have to go to school,* she thought. *If I want to be a writer, I need an education.* With this, she fell asleep.

# 2
# To the Hospital

There were more days of adjustment at the new school. But there were a few good days too.

One morning Ruth Ann heard the click of the door as Daddy left for work. She dragged her eyes open with an effort. She had to get up and do her own hair and open, comb out, and rebraid the hair of each sister. Terry would do the lunches. Ruth Ann couldn't afford to buy food in the cafeteria as the other students did; so she still carried her lunch. Mamma still wasn't well; so they let her sleep in whenever possible.

Ruth Ann braided her hair and wound the dark coils automatically around her head. She wondered what it would be like to take a pair of scissors and cut off the braids with a few well-aimed snips. Louella with the gimlet eyes always had new remarks about Ruth Ann's hair style and prayer covering.

Ruth Ann had asked her mother about cutting her hair. "No," Mamma had said. "You know what the Bible teaches."

Roxy Davidson was still her best friend, but she had added others since. At first she had thought they liked her only because she could help them with their English lessons. One day she realized that some students she'd never helped smiled at her in the hall. Maybe they liked her for herself. She was not sure.

Ruth Ann finished pinning up her braids and shook her sisters. "Come on, Janice, I know you're just pretending to be asleep." Janice put her pudgy arm over her face and groaned. Ruth Ann knew Jan wouldn't get up for at least another ten minutes.

Terry was no problem. She always got right up and started work on the lunches. Little Donna always rebelled. Sometimes Ruth Ann felt like letting her miss the bus and stay home by herself for a day. Maybe she would learn a lesson. Her sisters called Donna "cow tail" because she was always the very last one ready no matter where they were going.

Downstairs Terry clattered lunch boxes and jars in her hurry to finish the job. "Sh!" Ruth Ann warned. "Let's not wake Mamma if we can help it." She cleared away Daddy's breakfast things. He never managed to do that before he left for work at six.

Just then Ruth Ann heard Mamma call in a queer, tight voice, "Ruth Ann, come quickly!"

She dashed to the bedroom door. Mamma was a quiet heap on the bed, her face gray, her lips a sickly shade of blue. "What's wrong, Mamma?" Ruth Ann gasped.

"Ruth Ann, get Daddy." Mamma's lips moved and

Ruth Ann caught the feeble words.

"Yes, Mamma, I'll go right away." She started for the car, calling over her shoulder to her sisters, "Girls, Mamma is sick; I'm going for help."

Ruth Ann started the old Chevy with a lurch. She was pretty sure of the gears now, but she usually ripped them. The country road leading to the place where Daddy worked was all dirt.

*It's a good thing Daddy taught me to drive,* she thought. *We really should have a telephone, living back in the woods like this, but Daddy keeps saying we can't afford it now, maybe later we'll get one.*

Ruth Ann drove as fast as she dared. The old car seemed to hit all the potholes, shaking Ruth Ann until her stomach churned. She stopped with a jerk at the house Daddy was repairing. She saw him on the roof and ran to the corner of the house.

"Daddy!" she shouted. "Come home right away. Mamma's awful sick." She saw her father's face pale under its usual ruddiness and thought for one dreadful moment he was going to fall off the roof. Then he straightened and started backing down the ladder. Ruth Ann watched him run to the old pickup he drove to work and start off with a roar.

She stood there for a moment, feeling a cold chill sweep her body. *You dunce,* she thought, *you should not have told him when he was on the roof. What are you trying to do, lose both your parents in one day?*

*Hurry, Daddy, hurry,* she thought, remembering how Mamma had looked.

Driving home swiftly, she arrived just in time to see Daddy half leading, half carrying Mamma to the

14

pickup. Seeing the car, he brought Mamma toward it instead. Ruth Ann opened the door and Daddy helped Mamma in. "We're going to the doctor, Ruth Ann," he said hastily. "Get the girls to school if you can, and don't forget to pray. Pray for your mamma." He almost choked on the last words.

Ruth Ann watched the car dusting down the road, then hurried back to the house. She still had all the girls' hair to open, comb out, and rebraid. Her sisters huddled together on the battered old sofa. Donna's chocolate brown eyes were almost black with fright. Terry sat motionless, her hand gripping Janice's for comfort. Janice had her eyes closed; Ruth Ann guessed she was praying.

After one glance at her sisters, Ruth Ann knew she mustn't cry or they all would. Somehow she would have to find the courage to get them to school. They would be better off there.

Ruth Ann swallowed hard and said, "Come on, girls, we've got to get ready for school. Janice, you finish the lunches. Terry, open your braids, and I'll help Donna with hers."

The girls stared at her in amazement. "You mean we're going to school even when Mamma's so sick?" asked Donna.

"Yes, what would we do here all day?" Ruth Ann stripped the rubber bands from Donna's hair and swiftly opened her tousled braids. To Janice, who seemed unable to move, she said, "Hurry, Janice. The bus stops in fifteen minutes." Janice unfroze and ran to the kitchen to wrap sandwiches.

Ruth Ann had never combed hair so fast. She rebraided the three girls' hair in seven minutes. Then

15

they all grabbed lunches and books and ran down the lane.

The bus was almost to their stop, and Ruth Ann raced ahead of her sisters to flag it. Behind her, Donna screamed. Looking back, Ruth Ann saw her sprawled in the dust. "I'm bleeding to death," Donna wailed. She had fallen, and a thin trickle of blood stained her knee. Terry, wheezing asthmatically, ran back and lifted Donna to her feet. The bus driver saw Ruth Ann's waving arms and stopped. Janice pulled feverishly at her knee socks, which had fallen all the way to her ankles.

Ruth Ann pushed her sisters into the bus and sank into a seat with a sigh of exhaustion. They made it! She could have relaxed if she hadn't been aware of muffled giggles behind her.

Then she remembered Mamma and wondered what the doctor would say. She wondered how she would survive the day, not knowing what was wrong, but knowing it must be something terrible. So she quietly prayed on the way to school.

In history class Mrs. Connors asked the students "In what year did the Puritans sail to the New World?" No one answered immediately; so she said, "Ruth Ann, do you know?"

Ruth Ann, jerked into the present by hearing her name, tried to remember the question. It had something to do with sailing for America—must have been what year Columbus sailed for America. "Fourteen-ninety-two," she said brightly.

The class roared with laughter. "If you were trying to be funny, you failed completely," scolded Mrs. Conners.

"I'm sorry," Ruth Ann bowed her head, ashamed. She longed to get home. She simply couldn't concentrate on lessons.

Latin class was almost as bad as history. It was Ruth Ann's turn to read, and she'd lost track of where the class was reading. Looking at the page, she began where she thought the other student had stopped. She read a sentence and translated it.

"That's fine," Mrs. Conners said. "The only trouble is that Ronny just finished translating that very same sentence. Come down from the clouds, young lady!" Ruth Ann was saved from further embarrassment by the ringing of the last bell.

*Oh, it's time to go home.* Already she felt better.

She met her sisters on the bus. They all looked tired and worried. "Did you hear anything about Mamma?" they asked.

"No. We'll just have to wait till we get home," Ruth Ann told them.

Each hill seemed longer than usual that evening. Ruth Ann thought her books had never seemed so heavy. The girls looked for the car the moment they got over the last hill. Ruth Ann sighed. The car was still gone. Daddy wasn't home yet.

A stillness hung over the house. Janice silently stacked the breakfast dishes. Terry and Donna opened their books and tried to study. Ruth Ann got potatoes from the basement and pared them for supper.

Then they heard the unmistakable sound of the old Chevy climbing up the hill. As they rushed out the door to meet the car, they saw immediately that Mamma wasn't along.

"Where's Mamma?" screamed Donna before Daddy could get out of the car.

When she saw her father's face, Ruth Ann dreaded hearing the answer. Daddy had always been noted for his boyish appearance, but Ruth Ann noticed for the first time the tiny bits of gray in his hair and the lines of anxiety on his forehead. He looked at his daughters for a moment, then said heavily, "Your mother is in the hospital, girls."

# 3
# Dark Times

"What's wrong with her?" Donna's voice piped shrilly.

Daddy sat down at the kitchen table, looking tired. "She was hemorrhaging, and the doctor says she's anemic and will have to be in the hospital for a long time. But she'll probably be all right."

Ruth Ann sighed. Daddy had said "probably" This left her mind filled with doubts. She thought too of the mountains of work stretching before her. Hiring help was an impossibility. Daddy's carpenter jobs were too uncertain, and now there would be hospital bills. Ruth Ann wished she could stop thinking about it, but she couldn't. As the eldest daughter, she would be in charge. Her sisters were not old enough to help very much. What would she make for supper?

"I guess you'll have to be our mamma now," Donna said. She was worried too.

"Yes, I guess so," agreed Ruth Ann. Then a thought hit her. She might have to leave school if she couldn't keep things going otherwise. The thought was not unattractive; she still had moments of wanting to choke Louella. But there was Roxy— Roxy, so kind and understanding. And Roxy had introduced her to Cindy Jackson, a blue-eyed, vivacious brunette. Cindy was very friendly to Ruth Ann. She noticed that Cindy didn't mind copying from other students if she didn't know the answers, but then all people had some faults.

But she couldn't drop out of school. She had vowed for years that she would graduate from high school. She needed an education if she wanted to be a writer. Sometimes she wasn't sure that was what she wanted to be. She had moments of despair when she was sure she could never write anything really worthwhile. *But I must finish school,* she told herself.

The next morning she was up at six o'clock, doing laundry in the basement. While she watched the clothes swishing in the old wringer washer, she recited a line that she wanted to remember for biology. When the first load had finished washing, she bent over the wringer and pushed the steaming clothes into it as fast as she could. *I hope it keeps working,* she worried between biological axioms.

Sometimes the wringer wouldn't work, and she had to wring things by hand. She shivered as she plunged the clothes up and down in the cold rinse water. Then she put the clothing through the wringer again and lifted the heavy basket of laundry. Her arms ached as she carried the basket to the wash line.

She hung the clothes as far as she could from

the tree at the end of the line. If it rained, the drops
from the tree would be sooty and the clothes would
all have to be washed again. She looked at the lead-
en sky and prayed, *Dear God, please don't let it
rain today.* Then in shame she added, *Unless You
really think we need it.*

After that there were three heads to comb. Ruth
Ann left the lunches to Terry that morning. Donna
couldn't find her books and had to be dragged wail-
ing down the lane so that they wouldn't miss their
bus. Terry yelled back at Donna, "Hurry up, cow
tail!"

Just as they reached the bus the rain began falling
in huge drops. Ruth Ann looked in dismay at the
clouds. The laundry would probably be wet and dripping when they got home.

At school, although Ruth Ann tried to concentrate
on her lessons, she kept seeing dripping sheets and
wondering how the family would sleep that night.
The Millers had no money for spare sheets. *I guess
we'll just have to sleep on the quilts,* she thought.
She jerked suddenly and came back to reality when
Mrs. Jensen brushed her shoulder as she went by the
desk. She looked at Ruth Ann's blank sheet of paper
and frowned.

"What's wrong with you today, Ruth Ann? You
don't usually have any trouble writing compositions,
do you?" She looked more closely at Ruth Ann's
face and saw her tired eyes. Her brusque tone softened and she asked, "What is it, Dear?"

Ruth Ann felt a sudden longing to confide in someone, but this wasn't the time. Everyone was looking
at her; so she just shook her dark head, bent her face

22

intently over her paper, and began to write. Mrs. Jensen moved on up the aisle, shaking her head.

In biology Ruth Ann found she hadn't studied hard enough for her test. She seemed to have forgotten all she had learned. The letters on the test sheet danced out of focus. She clutched her pencil between shaking fingers. *I'm going to fail this test. I know I am. I'll never get through school like this.*

While she tried to think of answers, she saw baskets of ironing and piles of dirty laundry in her mind. She could see herself trying to get supper every evening while her homework lay neglected on her desk. She saw a report card filled with C's and D's and suddenly felt the weight of complete despair.

For a moment she rested her head on her hand and closed her eyes. *Oh, dear God, help me. I just can't do it all alone. You know all about it; please help me to bear it, or send someone to help me.*

When Ruth Ann lifted her head, weak sunlight was falling on her paper. She looked out and saw small patches of blue sky. Maybe it would clear off and the wash would dry after all. Ruth Ann half smiled and set to work at furious speed on her test.

Her mind seemed clearer, and she found that she knew more answers than she had before. She handed in her paper, hoping for at least a C. She knew she wouldn't be able to make straight A's as she had before. Making passing grades was the important thing now.

That evening, as they walked up the hill together, Janice groaned, "Oh, think of all that work to do at home! I didn't even get the breakfast dishes washed."

"I'm glad it's your turn to wash," Donna said. "I

did them last evening."

"No, you didn't, I did," Terry corrected.

"You did not—" and the quarrel was on. The two girls wrangled all the way to the top of the hill. Ruth Ann listened with half an ear. She had her own problems to think about.

That night Ruth Ann sat in the kitchen doing her homework. Her sisters had all gone to bed. She looked at the clock and saw that it was already past twelve. Although the family slept on unironed sheets, the other ironing had taken much longer than she thought it should. She longed to play the piano to release some of the tension that made her hands clench into fists, but everyone else was sleeping.

She closed her book with a small thud. Her eyes were no longer focusing.

Upstairs she dashed cold water on her face. Feeling slightly refreshed, she wrote in her journal. "Things are very bad. If only Mamma were here! My grades are going to suffer, I know. No more A's for me except in English class. I could do fine in English even if I were forced to stand on my head, but algebra will probably get me down."

Ruth Ann capped her pen and slid *Dramatic Events*, her journal, under her mattress. Her secret thoughts about Brian, her boy ideal, were recorded in the journal and could not be trusted to snoopy sisters' eyes. Drusilla, her pen, found its place on the bedside stand.

*Dramatic Events* had to suffer through all her trials, and Drusilla was her steadfast green-inked friend. Sometimes Ruth Ann spent hours "writing it out." Then, free of anger or whatever emotion had

24

driven her to her journal, she found she could endure life again.

Now she was too tired to write more. She set her alarm for five, noting that it was already one o'clock. The mending would be waiting for her inexperienced hands in the morning. She had never done the mending before. That was one thing Mamma hadn't taken time to teach her how to do. *Oh, God, help me somehow,* she prayed, and fell into tired sleep.

With passing days reports from the hospital did not improve. Mamma was holding her own, but no more.

Ruth Ann battled constantly against stacks of laundry, ironing, and mending. Daddy made pathetic attempts to help during the little time he had at home. Ruth Ann had to laugh at the crooked patch he sewed on the jagged tear in his trousers. The younger girls were a lot of help, although there were times when Ruth Ann had to rewash greasy dishes.

At school her papers were coming back with C's on them. A sense of failure shadowed each day. She was not doing her best work at home or in school. She would have to become accustomed to the cold stares of her teachers who expected good work from her, for she could not tell them about her problems at home. That would be asking for sympathy, which she would not do. She had told only Roxy and Cindy about her mother's illness. They both understood and tried to help her with her studies.

# 4
# Cheater

Algebra was the worst problem. Although Ruth Ann tried until her mind swarmed with the little dancing demons, she could not understand numbers. When she had had more time to study, she could manage. Now she was at the point of giving up; but she knew if she stopped trying, she would hardly pass the course. She had never failed any class before. It would break Mamma's and Daddy's hearts if she failed. They were proud of her straight-A record.

When the day of the big algebra test came, Cindy asked, "Are you ready for the test?"

"No, I don't think I'll ever be ready. I'll probably fail the course." Ruth Ann leaned her head on her hand and closed her eyes for a moment. She had been up until one the night before trying to study. That morning she had forced herself to get up at five and do the laundry. Pain gnawed at her back and knifed her legs. She longed to rest her aching body on the tiled floor of the schoolroom if only for a moment.

"You look beat." Cindy stared at the dark circles

beneath Ruth Ann's eyes and noted that her dress belt was so loose that it hung limply from her body. "Are you sure you shouldn't see a doctor?"

Roxy agreed, "You surely should, I'll bet you've lost six or eight pounds."

"Oh, fiddlesticks!" Ruth Ann turned away to hide her emotion. It was good to know they cared.

The bell rang and the girls went to algebra class. Ruth Ann's mouth went dry with fear and dread. Cindy sat down in front of her and flipped the pages of her text in final review. Ruth Ann watched her enviously. Math must have been revealed to her in her crib. She understood and loved it as Ruth Ann did English.

Cindy met her eyes and winked. Ruth Ann smiled. It was wonderful to have friends. She had a feeling Cindy understood, or at least tried to understand, the situation she was facing at home.

Mr. Bently came in, his arms loaded with test papers. Sudden chill gripped Ruth Ann. Mr. Bently's brown eyes could show anger and his usually kind, weather-beaten face could be stern. When he saw her completed test, it was possible that he would reprimand her before the entire class. She had been mistaken in letting Mr. Bently know that she was intelligent. He expected marvels from anyone who showed ability. He had already told her he was disappointed in her. How would he feel when she failed the test today?

Cindy turned and whispered softly, "Ruth Ann, I know you didn't have time to study. I'll keep my paper in plain sight. Copy my answers if you want to."

Horror showed on Ruth Ann's face. "You mean cheat?" she whispered back. Then she saw Mr. Bently's stern eyes at the front of the room and she subsided into silence.

"Put away your texts now. It's time for the test." Mr. Bently moved down the aisle, distributing tests. Ruth Ann took her paper, her hands clammy and cold. She scanned the sheet. Square roots, logarithms—dizziness dimmed her eyes. Even if she had studied, she doubted that she could have mastered all that. Without study, it was hopeless to attempt the first problem on the test. She wanted to run from the room and Mr. Bently's probing eyes.

In front of her, Cindy's pencil moved rapidly across the page. She would be through the test before the others were at the halfway point. Ruth Ann drew a doodle and scratched across it monotonously again and again. It would be so easy to copy Cindy's answers. Unlike some of the other students, Cindy was not bent over the paper, but sat erect and left her paper in the open.

Ruth Ann could not help seeing the answer to the first question. After that, she couldn't stop. The disappointment in Daddy's eyes if she failed the course would be too much to bear, she knew.

Her eyes glued themselves to Cindy's paper as her pencil moved quickly. Near the end of the test, she stopped. Someone was watching her. She was sure of it. A prickle of fear snaked across her back. She turned and looked straight into Louella Jones's small, unpleasant eyes. Louella always had something nasty to say about Mennonites in Ruth Ann's presence. Her tongue was as cutting as a razor. Most of the students tried to avoid her barbed remarks.

Ruth Ann dropped her pencil and stared at her test for the remainder of the class. She fought a wild desire to tear her paper into shreds. Mr. Bently would never understand such behavior. How could she explain to him that she had cheated and needed a new test? At any rate she would probably remember the answers she had already copied. Miserably she covered her eyes with her hands.

Mr. Bently stopped by her desk and picked up her paper. Glancing quickly across her answers, he said, "I'm glad to see you are getting back into the swing of things, Ruth Ann."

Ruth Ann wanted to shout at him, *I'm not; I never will either.* Her brown eyes were stormy with misery and frustration.

After class Ruth Ann walked sadly down the corridor. Louella Jones was waiting for her at the corner. "Cheater," she hissed. Ruth Ann walked faster to escape Louella's hateful eyes. *Oh, why had she let temptation overcome her?*

At home that evening she wrote in her journal, "I have done a terrible thing. I stole Cindy's brains in algebra class. How could I do it?" Drusilla dropped green tears across the confession. Ruth Ann blotted the page and closed the book.

"What are you doing?" Donna asked from the bed. Ruth Ann turned startled eyes to her small sister. "Are you worried?"

"I thought you were asleep, Donna. Don't worry, things will work out somehow."

Donna's chocolate eyes frowned in unbelief. "I wonder sometimes whether they will. When will

Mamma ever come back? I've asked God dozens of times to make her well. He must not be listening."

*I'm sure He won't listen to me now,* thought Ruth Ann, her sin standing between her and God like a solid black wall. Aloud she said, "Go to sleep, Donna. Tomorrow is another day." She slid her journal under the mattress beyond the reach of Donna's eyes. Someday her sisters would discover her hiding place. Perhaps they knew it now.

She turned off the light and closed her eyes hopefully. Sleep would be long in coming with such a weight of guilt on her mind.

# 5

# The Struggle

The next day Ruth Ann went wearily back to school. What else was there to do? She vowed to complete her high school education.

At school Louella was standing in front of her locker door. "Aha, I know something about you," Louella snickered. "What would you do if I told Mr. Bently? Things could be pretty bad for you." Seeing Ruth Ann cringe, she went on, "Tell you what—I'll make a deal with you. We've got a big English test tomorrow. I sit behind you in class. If you let me copy from you, I won't tell."

Ruth Ann lifted her hand to slap Louella's face. Then her hand dropped limply. Louella had a right to think that she would cheat again since she had done it once. She turned and walked away without a word.

Louella called after her, "You'll be sorry, Miss Priss."

That evening Ruth Ann went with Daddy to see Mamma at the hospital. Her sisters stayed in the car.

They were within sight from the window. It was the first time Ruth Ann had gone to see her mother since Mrs. Miller had been hospitalized.

She peeped in the door before she went in. Mamma's eyes were closed. The little oxygen tube taped to her nose sent a thrill of anxiety through Ruth Ann. Daddy hadn't mentioned that Mamma was still under oxygen. Ruth Ann gulped once or twice to clear her throat of the lump forming there. She would be cheerful for Mamma's sake.

As she walked over to the bed, Mamma opened her dark eyes and smiled weakly when she saw her. "It's my big girl," she said. She put out a hand, "How are things?" Mamma asked.

"OK," Ruth Ann managed to say. She could not trouble Mamma with her burdens.

"School?" questioned Mamma.

"Could be worse." Ruth Ann could not keep the grimness out of her tone.

Mamma squeezed her hand. "I'll get home somehow," she murmured and closed her eyes again.

Ruth Ann stood there holding her hand helplessly for a moment. Then she stooped and lightly touched her lips to Mamma's forehead. "We're all right, Mamma, but we miss you," she whispered and hurried from the room.

She stood in the hall for a minute, hands clasped, trying to regain some sort of control. How could things get any worse? With Donna, she felt that God had not been listening. Now with her guilty heart, she could not even pray. She bit her lip until the salty taste of blood filled her mouth.

In the car her sisters clamored for news of Mamma.

"How is she? Did she talk to you?"

"Yes, she says she'll be back with us sometime."
Ruth Ann tried to put an assurance into her voice
that she was far from feeling. For the first time she
faced the fact that Mamma might not come back. She
would not let herself think further. For her sisters'
sake she dared not show her fear.

On Sunday Ruth Ann automatically got ready for
church. She put on her prettiest dress in a false attempt at gaiety.

In Sunday school Brian sat beside her. She looked
forward to seeing Brian in church because she seldom
saw him anywhere else. He had asked her for dates
several times, but Daddy had always said, "No, wait
until you're sixteen."

She sat very still while the offering was being

taken. She did not want to break the spell of Brian's nearness. When she looked up, Brian's blue eyes met hers. Somehow today she could not bear the honesty of his gaze. She dropped her eyes.

Brian leaned toward her and whispered, "You look beautiful." She could not help smiling at that. Then she sobered. She was worthy of no one's admiration. Maybe the exterior was lovely, but beneath it lay something shabby and cowardly. What would Brian think if he knew that she had cheated?

Suddenly Ruth Ann knew what she must do. She would tell Mr. Bently and take the consequences. A failing grade would be preferable to the agony she was enduring. Louella had said she might tell Mr. Bently. Ruth Ann doubted that she really would, but she would keep the information poised like a club over Ruth Ann's head forever if she could. It would be good to look directly into Louella's small eyes and say, *I have already told him.*

With the decision, Ruth Ann once more felt calm and happy inside. It was so good to communicate with God again. *Oh, God, help me now to do what I have planned,* she prayed.

Next day Louella was waiting for her by Mrs. Jensen's door. "Well?" she asked.

"I can't let you copy from me," Ruth Ann said.

"Have you forgotten what I said I'd do?" A smug confidence lay on Louella's face.

"No, but I've thought of something better," Ruth Ann informed her. "I'm going to tell Mr. Bently myself."

"I don't believe it," Louella said flatly.

"Wait and see." Ruth Ann stared into Louella's

eyes until the other girl lowered her gaze and walked away, confused.

At lunch time, Ruth Ann went directly to Mr. Bently's room. He ate lunch on the first shift; so he was likely to be in his room.

The old gentleman looked up, surprise widening his eyes. "I was just thinking about you," he said, smiling. "You did so much better on your last test. I want to commend you."

Ruth Ann felt her ears burn. "That's why I came to see you. I hate to tell you this. I'm so ashamed."

"Why? Your test paper was very good. Cindy is the only one who made a better grade than you did."

"You're making it very hard for me, but I must tell you that I copied Cindy's work." Ruth Ann clasped and unclasped her hands.

Mr. Bently stared at her. "You don't mean that? How could you do such a thing? I'm sure you knew better than that. I thought Mennonites were always honest."

Ruth Ann hadn't thought of that angle. She had even disgraced her church. She bent her head and clenched her hands. Mr. Bently looked at her more closely.

"You're trembling, Ruth Ann. I've noticed you don't look at all well lately." His tone softened, and Ruth Ann almost choked. She would far rather have him shout at her. It would be easier for her to keep calm.

"Is there trouble at home or something?"

"My mother has been very ill. I have to keep house." Ruth Ann tried to keep her tone matter-of-fact, but her lower lip trembled slightly.

The old gentleman patted her shoulder. "I'm very

35

sorry to hear that, Ruth Ann. I think I see why you did it. This is a hard subject, and you haven't had time to study. Were you afraid of failing the course?"

Ruth Ann gulped. "Yes," she said.

"Well, I'll have to give you a failing mark for the test, but I think you will not fail the course. Maybe things will get better at home, and you'll have more time to study?"

"Thank you." Ruth Ann left the room. Overwhelming relief made her feel weak. She had told Mr. Bently herself. Now when she saw Louella, her mind would be clear of guilt.

*Oh, God, thank You for giving me the courage to do it,* she prayed.

She walked up the hill that evening with her sisters. Their chatter floated harmlessly about her. She wondered how Mamma was today. She dared to hope that things might soon take a turn for the better.

At the top of the hill she paused. "Whose car is that, girls?" she asked.

"Isn't it Aunt Etta's?" Donna's eyes shone at the thought of the treat in store. Aunt Etta was their favorite aunt.

"I think it is." Terry started running.

Janice looked about, puzzled. "Didn't you hang up the laundry this morning, Ruth Ann?"

"I certainly did." Ruth Ann could see that the laundry was no longer on the lines. "Bless Aunt Etta's dear heart. I'll bet she took it down for me. She's always doing nice things for people."

"Maybe she'll read me a story," suggested Donna and skipped her way toward the house.

36

When Ruth Ann came into the living room, her eyes widened in delight. Aunt Etta had cleaned and dusted until even the shabby furniture seemed to shine. She could hear the clatter of dishes in the kitchen. Aunt Etta washed dishes in record time.

Ruth Ann walked slowly into the kitchen. Aunt Etta looked at her niece in compassion. "I was at the hospital to see your mother after lunch. I didn't realize before that you were doing all the work. I should have thought of it without having to be told."

"How is Mamma?" Ruth Ann asked eagerly.

"She took a turn for the better today." Aunt Etta smiled at Ruth Ann's happy face.

"Why don't you go and play the piano? I'll do some of this work. I'm staying for a few days. After I go, I'll plan to pick up the laundry and do the ironing."

"Oh, but isn't that too much for you?" Ruth Ann could not believe her ears.

"No, I don't have much to do. Without children, I really have too much time on my hands. Besides, I just got a new washer and dryer."

"That's wonderful." Ruth Ann sighed blissfully. She went into the living room and ran her fingers experimentally across the piano keys. *I'm so rusty,* she thought. *I must practice more. Now since Aunt Etta is taking over, maybe I can begin to live again instead of just existing. And maybe, just maybe, I can catch up in school and make some decent grades again.*

She played a lilting melody, feeling her spirits lift with the gaiety of the music.

She had often wanted to be grown up, but now she found great comfort in the fact that Aunt Etta was taking over.

# 6

# The
# Slumber
# Party

Ruth Ann walked with slumping shoulders down the hall. It had been a particularly rough day. The biology test had been especially hard, and in the hall she had overheard Louella Jones making one of her pointed remarks about Mennonites. Louella had meant her to hear. Of that she was sure.

"Wait up, Ruth Ann." Ruth Ann turned to see Roxy Davidson following her. The two girls fell into step. "Ruth Ann, I'm having a slumber party tomorrow evening. Would you like to come?"

Ruth Ann brightened. She smiled into Roxy's dancing green eyes. Just looking at Roxy made her feel better.

"I'd love to, Roxy, but Mother's still in the hospital. She's getting better, but I have to stay with the kids. Maybe, though, I could get my Aunt Etta to stay for one night."

"Good, I'll count on that."

"Who else is coming?" Ruth Ann asked.

Roxy began naming the crowd, counting them off

on her fingers. When she got to number ten, she finished, "Louella Jones."

Ruth Ann tried to check a sigh. "I know," Roxy said, "she isn't very nice. But I think having friends would help her a lot."

"I suppose you're right." Ruth Ann often marveled at how well Roxy understood everyone.

That evening Ruth Ann called Aunt Etta, who agreed to come over the next night. In the morning Ruth Ann packed her overnight bag while Donna and Terry looked on in delight. "I wish I could be grown up right now." Donna sighed in envy. "You're not staying more than one night, are you?" Donna's chocolate-colored eyes lit with anxiety. "Who is going to read my bedtime story?"

"Oh, Janice can do that," soothed Ruth Ann. It wouldn't hurt Donna to do without her big sister for one night.

"But she doesn't read as long as you do," protested Donna.

"Good, then you'll get up earlier in the morning instead of being the cow tail." Ruth Ann went on packing, ignoring Donna's glares.

"All right, I just hope you don't come back." Donna flounced off the bed and went to search for her school books, a chore that commonly occupied most of her time before the bus came.

"Are those girls nice where you're going tonight?" asked Terry.

"Yes, some of them are very nice." Ruth Ann clicked shut her bag and hurried downstairs to make sure the lunches were packed and all the braids done satisfactorily.

On the way to school she couldn't help worrying about Louella Jones. Louella would be certain to have some catty remark to make. She hadn't forgotten the cheating episode.

*I can take just so much and no more,* Ruth Ann thought. *I hope she doesn't test me beyond my endurance.* For a moment she felt like telling Roxy she couldn't go after all. But she couldn't disappoint Roxy. Besides, she really wanted a chance to spend more time with her friends.

That evening all the girls piled into Roxy's bus, some of them standing in the aisle. Ruth Ann was fortunate enough to find a seat. She noticed that Louella walked past, without glancing at her. Then Roxy came in and sat beside Ruth Ann. "I'm so glad you could come," Roxy smiled.

"We'll have lots of fun this evening," Roxy went on. "I'd like you to help with the cooking. I'm sure you're a good cook. I'm planning to make spaghetti for one thing."

"Oh, good. I love spaghetti!" Ruth Ann felt her fears slipping away as she listened to Roxy's chatter.

At Roxy's house they were soon busy with all the little jobs Roxy assigned them. Roxy's mother was out for the evening, and her father was working in the shop. Roxy and Ruth Ann worked side by side, mixing meatballs. Ruth Ann thought she felt someone staring at her.

"Hum, the Mennonite cook!" Louella's sharp voice was audible even when she muttered. Ruth Ann felt her ears grow hot, and bit back an angry retort. Why couldn't Louella mind her own business? Ruth Ann wanted to turn and glare at Louella, but even without seeing the pest she could imagine how Louella looked. Her forehead would wear a frown and a sneer would mar her narrowed eyes and unhappy mouth. Her shoulders would be drawn back haughtily to add to her short stature. Her clothing would be just a bit rumpled and ill-fitting as usual. Ruth Ann felt something akin to hatred boiling inside her as she thought about Louella and all the unkind things she had done.

*Stop it,* she told herself. *Maybe she can't help herself. Maybe she's only trying to draw attention to herself.*

Ruth Ann finished mixing the meatballs and dropped them one by one into the sizzling oil. Saliva pooled in her mouth as the delicious aroma rose from the frying chunks of meat.

When the girls sat down to eat, Louella reached at once for the salad and began helping herself. Roxy waited until she had finished, then said quietly, "Let's bow our heads while Ruth Ann says grace."

Ruth Ann prayed simply as she had been taught to do. The room was very quiet after she had finished. Then Louella giggled unpleasantly, "I guess it's a good thing we have a Mennonite here to do our praying. None of us know how." She looked about with a quick jerking motion of her head, waiting for everyone to join the laughter. But none of the girls so much as smiled.

"Maybe we can't pray as well as Ruth Ann." Roxy's face was sober. "But I'm sure we pray; at least I do." Several of the other girls nodded their heads. An uncomfortable flush rose in Louella's sallow cheeks. Ruth Ann was amazed to find herself

41

feeling pity for the girl. Louella had succeeded only in making a spectacle of herself. Her joke had fallen flat.

Later, as the girls prepared for bed, Louella tried again. Ruth Ann let down her long hair; she had worn it in a bun that day. Linda Jane gasped as the dark cloud tumbled about Ruth Ann's shoulders. Louella was ready with a quick remark. "Well, look at the little saint. I'll bet she's never cut her hair. That doesn't keep her from cutting corners on algebra tests, though."

Roxy turned to Louella in exasperation. "Oh, really, Louella! You make me tired. Can't you ever let Ruth Ann alone? Everyone makes a mistake sometimes. If you don't stop, I think I'll have my father drive you home."

For once Louella seemed completely squelched. She dropped her small eyes and said nothing. Ruth Ann felt a prickle of joy at seeing her subdued, yet that spark of pity returned an instant later.

"Maybe Louella just doesn't understand," Ruth Ann said. She hesitated, then forced herself to go on. "Perhaps I should explain a bit. I'm not trying to set myself up as someone better than anybody else by dressing as I do. Probably if I'd been raised in any of your homes, I'd look just as you do. I dress and do my hair the way I do because this is what I was taught by my parents. You all know I'm human, even though no one has mentioned the cheating episode except Louella. I know God will help me to do better. I want you all to be my friends." As Ruth Ann finished, the girls came to her and said they wanted to be friends, too—all except Louella.

42

Louella kept to herself for the rest of the evening. When everyone was finally ready for bed, Louella was still sitting dejectedly on a vanity bench. Roxy took pity on her and said, "Come on, Louella, don't you want to see the new dress I got for church?"

The girls all exclaimed about the new dress. Then Roxy pulled out another dress. "Here's an old one. I never did care much for it. If one of you would like to have it, you're certainly welcome to it."

Ruth Ann saw Louella's thin hands reaching for the dress eagerly. "Oh, Roxy, it's lovely. I want it." Ruth Ann's mind traveled swiftly across the days she had known Louella. No, Louella didn't have nice clothing. This would probably be the first nice dress she'd ever had. Ruth Ann watched Louella's fingers caress the dress and thought, *There's something underneath her snippy personality.* At that moment she decided to keep on trying to win Louella's friendship.

# 7
# Mamma's Return

Mamma had been in the hospital exactly four weeks when Daddy came home with the great news. The girls met him in the yard and knew at once that something good had happened. His shoulders were erect, his hazel eyes happy and alive once more.

"What is it, Daddy? Is Mamma coming home?"

Daddy nodded. Donna and Terry skipped around their father in their gaiety, while Janice, beginning to feel her maturity, merely stood with shining eyes. Ruth Ann felt relief at first, and then a kind of panic.

What would her mother think of her housekeeping? Of course, Aunt Etta had done some of it, but Ruth Ann still felt responsible. And what was it Daddy was telling the girls right now?

"Girls," he was saying, "you'll have to be careful about making noise. Mamma has been pretty sick, and she can't stand a lot of racket." Ruth Ann's mind went back to the one day she had visited Mamma in the hospital. She could still see the sickly pallor of Mamma's skin and hear her saying, "Please don't stand too close, Ruth Ann. I can't breathe very well."

"What time will you bring Mamma home?" Donna hopped about on one foot, reminding Ruth Ann of a jumping jack.

"She'll be released just after lunch," Daddy said. "Since you girls don't have school today, you'll see her as soon as we get home."

"Well, we'd better get the house cleaned up." Ruth Ann started for the house. "We want everything to be in order when Mamma gets here."

Ruth Ann assigned some cleaning to each of her sisters. It seemed no time at all till everything was finished, and all they had to do was sit and wait to hear the old Chevy grinding up the hill.

Donna impatiently twirled the piano stool. "Why don't they hurry up and get here?" She thumped the keys, crashing heavily on the bass section.

"Stop that, Donna." Ruth Ann knew her voice was edgy, but Donna would have to learn to be quiet.

Donna frowned. "Why should I? You play the piano, Ruth Ann."

"I may not be able to for a while." Ruth Ann felt suddenly empty as she realized that she might have to abandon her music for a time. Maybe Mamma would not like to hear her play anymore.

Janice said, "Oh, well, there are lots of other things to do. I'd much rather read a book anyway." She got up and reached for her book. She soon seemed absorbed in the story. Ruth Ann shook her head. Maybe reading was enough for Janice, but her life would never be complete without music.

*Well, it can't be forever,* she comforted herself. *I'll manage somehow.*

45

Terry sat quietly on the sofa, now and then rubbing her eyes. Ruth Ann looked at her long eyelashes and saw that they were wet with tears. She sat down beside her sister and put an arm around her. "What's wrong, Terry?" she asked softly.

Terry caught her breath with a sob. "It's just that I missed Mamma so much." She leaned against her sister, and Ruth Ann felt a lump in her own throat. It is hard for young girls to do without a mother.

Then all the girls straightened as they heard the car at last. Donna flew out the door, her brown legs leaping down the walk. For once she was not the "cow tail." The others weren't far behind, with Ruth Ann cautioning, "Now remember what Daddy said about being quiet."

Daddy drove carefully up by the house. "Now lean on me," Ruth Ann heard him say. When she could bring herself to look, she saw Mamma, leaning on Daddy's arm, taking small shaky steps. Mamma's face had grown drawn and thin, her tall body leaner by many pounds. The streaks of gray in her black hair had become larger. Dark shadows beneath her eyes made them look hollow, and her lips seemed drained of color.

The four sisters stood watching Mamma's short journey from car to house. Donna, for once, had nothing to say. Terry and Janice, tense and quiet, clasped each other's hands. Was this stranger really Mamma? Ruth Ann moved quickly to open the door.

Then Mamma was in the bedroom, sinking onto the bed with an exhausted sigh. She closed her eyes and Ruth Ann moved quickly from the room. She didn't want to weary Mamma with any conversation now.

She looked about the kitchen. What should she make for supper? She had put out a large roast to thaw the evening before. Maybe she should cook it and make a huge pot of vegetable soup as she had sometimes in the past. Mamma was fond of vegetable soup. Ruth Ann set about gathering all the ingredients.

She was peeling onions, trying to keep back the tears, when Terry and Donna burst into the kitchen. Only Ruth Ann's horrified protests kept them from rushing on into the living room.

"But, Ruthie, she has my ball," Donna protested.

"I don't care what she has. You are not to run in the house. Mamma has to have lots of rest and quiet." Ruth Ann frowned sternly at the flushed faces. It was going to be a chore to keep those two quiet. Janice was probably somewhere with a book. She would be no problem, but the other two? Ruth Ann shook her head in despair. What would she do? Then she remembered school, and thought guiltily that it would be a relief to get out of the house.

*It's not that I don't love my mother; it's just that it will be impossible to keep those girls quiet,* she thought.

After the soup was simmering on the stove, she sat down to play one of her new piano pieces. She fumbled over the first few chords, then dropped her hands heavily. She had forgotten, too. She was as bad as her sisters. For a despairing moment, she wanted to pound the keys regardless of Mamma's nerves. Then Mamma called from the bedroom.

Ruth Ann stood in the doorway, half frightened. Would Mamma scold her for playing the piano? Or

48

hadn't she cleaned the bedroom properly?

"Something smells so wonderful, Ruthie." Mamma's use of the little-girl name made Ruth Ann's eyes smart. "Are you cooking supper?" Mamma asked.

"Yes, vegetable soup."

Mamma's face lit with pleasure. "My favorite. It smells delicious. Would you bring me some as soon as it's finished?"

"Of course, Mamma."

Mamma leaned back against her pillows. "It's so good to be home. You have the house shining. I don't know what we'd do without you, Ruth Ann."

Ruth Ann could not hide her pride and pleasure. "Everybody helped, Mamma. We're so glad to have you home."

"When you're not busy, I wish you'd play something on the piano. I missed your playing so much when I was in the hospital."

Joy leaped into Ruth Ann's eyes. "You mean my playing won't upset you?"

"No, if you don't play noisy pieces, I won't mind. You've been keeping the girls so quiet, it's almost unnatural. Let them fight a little if they want to. It seems more like home."

Ruth Ann could feel the tiredness leaving all at once. Mamma was really home now; she still liked them just as they were. Now all was well.

# 8
# The
# World of
# Boys

For months Ruth Ann had longed for her sixteenth birthday. Every time Brian asked her to go out with him, she had to answer, "My father says not till I'm sixteen." Now suddenly her birthday was here. She knew that Brian would ask her to go out with him and she felt her heart do a flip at the thought. She wanted Brian to ask her; yet fear of the unknown dampened her eagerness.

There was no hiding the fact that she liked Brian. She had dreamed about him for years. He was her ideal of everything a boy should be. His sandy thatch of hair and long-lashed blue eyes delighted her. But what would they do on a date? What would they talk about? Would she be tongue-tied? Ruth Ann almost wished that she could postpone her birthday.

If only she had an older sister with whom to compare notes. Being the eldest daughter had its disadvantages. She could ask Mamma, but she felt a wave of shyness at the thought.

On the Sunday following her birthday, Ruth Ann

went to church with the family as usual. She and Brian sometimes sat together in Sunday school. This morning he was waiting for her, a broad grin on his face. "Happy birthday, Ruth Ann," he whispered to her.

"Thank you," she said, her heart pounding. She knew what he would say next. "Will you go out with me tonight?" he asked just as their teacher came in.

"I'll tell you after church," Ruth Ann said quickly and bent her dark head over her study guide.

She didn't hear much of the lesson. Usually Uncle Jim had no trouble keeping her attention, but this morning he just wasn't interesting.

During church Ruth Ann sat with her sisters and tried to listen to the sermon, but her eyes kept wandering across the church to Brian's broad back. She was glad she wasn't sitting beside him now. She couldn't have faced his penetrating eyes.

Brian was waiting for her outside after church. "You *are* giving me a rough time," he grumbled, but his eyes twinkled.

Ruth Ann felt a little more at ease. What was the matter with her anyway? Girls had to face that first date sometime. "Where will we go tonight?" she asked.

"I guess to young people's meeting," Brian said. His eyes sparkled. "You mean you're actually going with me?"

"All right, Brian, I'll go," Ruth Ann said, so softly that Brian bent to catch the words.

"I'll come for you at seven." Brian looked ready to conquer worlds as he strode across the church lawn.

*Now I've done it,* Ruth Ann thought. *Suppose I'm*

*a miserable failure as a date and he never asks me again? I'll feel just awful.*

At home after church, Ruth Ann cooked dinner. Mamma had still not regained her old strength. She helped with the dishes, though, and Ruth Ann took the opportunity to tell her about Brian.

"Mamma, Brian is taking me to church tonight," she said.

"Oh, that's nice. Brian seems like a very steady person." Mamma smiled. "Your first date, isn't it?"

"Yes." Ruth Ann absentmindedly swished soap over a dish. She spent the rest of the afternoon alternately reading a book and wondering what she and Brian would talk about that evening. Then it was time to get ready for church.

Ruth Ann put her hair up three times and took it down again. Donna was watching, amused and fascinated. "Say, you must like him a lot, or you wouldn't be so worried about your hair."

Ruth Ann nodded. "He's pretty nice, all right," she said. Donna was so small, she didn't mind her chatter.

"Does he like you, too?" Donna asked.

"Oh, I hope he does, I hope he does," Ruth Ann said fervently. She smoothed back the waves of her dark hair for the fourth time and set to work pinning up her braids again.

When she was through, Donna said, "You look pretty, Ruth Ann. I think Brian likes you, too. He always looks at you a lot in church."

Ruth Ann smiled. Sometimes Donna could be very comforting. Then she heard Brian drive up. She sat for a moment watching Brian get out of the car and come toward the house. She knew she should wait and make him think she wasn't ready. Wasn't that what girls always did? But she couldn't sit for a minute more. She ran down the stairs and met Brian at the door.

"Hi, Brian," she said as she opened the door. She had rehearsed this scene in her mind dozens of times. Now somehow she had forgotten all the extra flourishes she had rehearsed.

"Hello, Ruth Ann. All ready?" Brian asked. "We might as well go, don't you think?"

They walked to the car together, and he helped her into the car. How well he did everything!

Then they were on their own, shut up in the car together. Shyness wrapped Ruth Ann like a cloak. If only she could break the silence, she felt that things would be all right. She longed for Donna's quick wit to liven the scene. Unconsciously she clenched her hands.

Brian looked over and noted her anxiety. "Is something wrong, Ruth Ann? You do want to go to church with me, don't you?"

"Oh, yes, yes!" Ruth Ann's face came alive with feeling as she nodded at Brian.

"What are you doing in school now?" Brian wondered.

"Well, mostly I'm working on my research paper in English. Mrs. Jensen insists on perfection."

"She sounds like my teacher!" laughed Brian. "I was never able to earn more than a C in English. From what I hear, you're doing a lot better than that"

Ruth Ann smiled at his indirect praise. "I have to work hard, though," she said.

53

"Maybe that was my problem. I didn't take the time to try."

From Mrs. Jensen the conversation moved on to all phases of school life, and when they reached the church, Ruth Ann's hands lay calmly in her lap. Her dark eyes were bright with interest. *This isn't so frightening,* she thought, as they walked to the church.

When church was over, Brian drove her home. *Now what?* Ruth Ann wondered. *Do I ask him in, or will he say good night at the door?* If she did ask him in, would he like her home? With a thrust of regret she remembered the worn sofa and the thin carpet of the living room. She had a feeling Brian was accustomed to better things. *Oh, well,* she decided, *I'll invite him in. If he doesn't like our home, he needn't like me.*

"Will you come in?" she asked a little breathlessly as they paused at the front door.

"I'd like that very much." Ruth Ann felt a thrill of surprise at the pleasure in Brian's voice.

Inside the house she was at a loss for words. Should she offer refreshments? She remembered the cake and fruit left from dinner. "Would you care for something to eat, Brian?" she asked shyly. "Come on out to the kitchen and I'll find something!" she added.

*Boys are always hungry,* she thought, *and Brian is no exception.*

Brian started walking to the kitchen, then stopped as giggles came from upstairs. Ruth Ann glanced up the stairs and saw Donna's white-tailed nightie disappearing around the corner. "They should be in bed," she apologized.

Brian laughed. "They're cute. My brothers would do the same thing if you came to our house."

"That's right, you do have a lot of brothers, don't you? I think sisters are worse."

"I guess whatever you happen to have seems worse at the time." Ruth Ann set a plate of cake and fruit in front of Brian and was delighted when he ate every bit of it.

"That cake was good," he said. "I'll bet you baked it yourself, didn't you?"

"Yes," Ruth Ann admitted. "Cake baking is usually my job."

Brian looked at the clock. "I'd better go now. You'll have school in the morning." He unwound his long legs and started for the door.

Ruth Ann followed him, hoping wistfully that he would come again.

At the door Brian smiled down at her. "You're going to think I'm an awful pest, but will you go out with me again?"

Ruth Ann began to breathe again. "I'd like that," she said.

"I'll phone later," Brian promised.

Upstairs Ruth Ann watched the lights of the car fade into the darkness. She heard Donna's bare feet pattering up the hall. "Was he nice?" the little girl whispered.

"He's the very nicest boy in all the world." And Ruth Ann's heart sang with happiness.

# 9
## The Facts

Ruth Ann went out with Brian at least four times. She began to lose track of the times they'd been together. Brian had become a part of her life.

Ruth Ann was stimulated by their arguments. One evening when they were sitting in the living room, Brian asked, "Why do you wear your covering all the time?"

Stunned, Ruth Ann looked at him in silence. "You know very well why, Brian," she said at last. "You've been brought up in the same way I have."

Brian nodded and then said, "Things seem to be changing these days and some people don't believe the way they used to. That is the passage in 1 Corinthians."

Ruth Ann knew that Brian met many other girls in his school and even some in their own congregation. She was silent for a while, but she knew Brian needed an answer, an honest answer to what she believed and why.

"Brian," she began, "you know how I have been

taught by my parents. I can't just discard that teaching. I had to pray so often when Mother was in the hospital, when I had so much work to do at home. I prayed at home, in school, on the way to school, and it all helped so much."

Brian was silent and seemed to be looking straight ahead as he sat beside her. Finally he answered, "I wonder if we believe alike. I don't know. I have to think this out for myself, but I like you very much, Ruth Ann."

"You'd like if I'd cut my hair and wear it down like other girls, for example, shoulder length. Wouldn't you?" Ruth Ann asked.

Brian nodded silently.

Ruth Ann finally said, "It's what we believe that really counts after all, isn't it? If we live and think the way we believe, I know we will be happy."

When Brian continued the argument, Ruth Ann got up and walked away. "Must we talk about this, Brian?"

"No, of course not. Does it bother you?" Brian was beside her again, his eyes concerned.

"I'm sorry," she said.

"All right, let's forget it for now." Brian left soon afterward. Ruth Ann worried about their talk later. Had she made Brian angry? She wasn't sure.

The next Sunday morning in Sunday school class, Brian didn't say, "I'll see you tonight." Ruth Ann worried about it, yet she hoped he'd just forgotten and would call her later. When seven o'clock came and he hadn't phoned, Ruth Ann began to feel a dull throb in her head. She lay down in the room she shared with her sisters.

Donna came stamping in. "That Terry is the meanest thing. She won't play any games with me." Seeing Ruth Ann's closed eyes, she stopped grumbling and asked, "Where's Brian, Ruth Ann? Isn't he coming?"

"I don't know." The last thing in the world Ruth Ann wanted to do was answer questions about Brian. Maybe if she did something interesting, she would forget about him. Why not play with Donna? "Come on, Donna, I'll play games with you," she said.

The girls were halfway through a game of Chinese checkers when Daddy came in from his Sunday walk. "Why aren't you at church, Ruth Ann?" he asked.

Ruth Ann shook her head. "I didn't have any way to go," she said simply.

"What happened to Brian?"

"You tell me, and we'll both know," Ruth Ann snapped. She wanted to growl at someone, and Daddy was the nearest person.

"Sorry I asked," he said.

Ruth Ann looked miserably at her marbles. "Would you ask Terry to take my place, please?" she asked Donna. "I really don't feel very well."

Donna looked at her wisely. "You're sick because Brian didn't come, aren't you?" she asked. "I think he's a pretty mean guy to make you feel so bad."

Ruth Ann ran upstairs, not daring to reply to Donna's remark. It did seem that Brian owed her some sort of explanation after all these weeks. Ruth Ann sat staring into the darkness, hoping vainly to see the headlights of a car. She shook herself, wishing she could wake up. This all seemed like a very bad dream. She didn't even notice when Donna came in and climbed into bed.

Finally Ruth Ann went to bed, but not to sleep. She lay there beside Donna, thinking about Brian. She must have made him angry on their last date. Maybe he didn't care to date her anymore if she was so undecided about long hair and the covering. Maybe he'd rather date a girl who had cut her hair and didn't wear a prayer covering.

*Maybe, maybe, maybe*—her mind went on and on. Finally she fell into a troubled sleep.

All that week she wondered about Brian. Her dark eyes seemed to grow larger in her thin face. She disliked going to bed because she had trouble going to sleep.

The next Sunday Ruth Ann and her friend Mary were talking outside before the service began. "I noticed you weren't in church last Sunday evening," Mary remarked.

"Yes, do you know why?"

"Why?" Ruth Ann thought Mary looked guilty.

"Brian didn't call me." Ruth Ann could talk about it now. "I'm afraid he's mad at me. Did you hear anything about him?"

"No, I guess not." Mary was looking down at her shoes.

"Mary, you know something. I'm sure you do. Come on, tell me why Brian didn't take me to church."

Mary sighed. "Sometimes I wish I could comfortably tell a lie. All right, Ruth Ann, I do know something. My brother, Diz, saw Brian with Nelly Fisher at the Grove Church Mennonite Youth Fellowship. She's that girl who cut her hair, you know."

For a moment Ruth Ann seemed frozen. Her eyes stared glassily at Mary. "Stop that, Ruth Ann." Mary

60

shook her arm. "Say something."

"What am I supposed to say?" Ruth Ann asked numbly. "I should have known Brian wouldn't be interested in me for long. I think I know how he feels about long hair."

"Oh, well, it isn't the end of the world. There are other boys. I know plenty of fellows who would like to go out with you—long hair or not."

"Name one," Ruth Ann said.

"Well, Leonard is always looking at you. Diz says he's crazy about you."

"He reminds me of a cat waiting to be petted," Ruth Ann said cruelly. "Oh, it's no use, Mary; I just couldn't get interested in anyone else right now. Give me a little time to suffer first." She smiled at her weak attempt at humor.

"OK, but don't be too obvious about it. I wouldn't give Brian the satisfaction of knowing that he's broken your heart."

Ruth Ann straightened fiercely. "I'll be as happy as a jaybird. See if I'm not. You're right, I daren't let Brian see that I'm hurt. And if any other fellow asks me out, I'm going."

"That's the spirit," cheered Mary. "I knew you wouldn't let it get you down."

That afternoon Leonard phoned her. Ruth Ann suspected Mary had told him she wasn't going out with Brian that evening. When Leonard asked her whether he could come for her that evening, she forced herself to say yes in a pleased tone.

That evening she tried valiantly to enjoy herself. But Leonard kept agreeing with everything she said to him, until she wanted to scream. She longed for the

61

lively arguments she and Brian always had. Leonard reminded her more than ever of a well-behaved cat, his dark hair sleek, his ears neat against his head.

Hoping to get him to disagree with her, she asked, "Leonard, how would you like me if I cut my hair and wore it short?" Knowing that Leonard's mother always had her share to say about girls who bobbed their hair, Ruth Ann tried to suppress her smile.

Leonard's face remained placid. "I'd like that—you would look nice with short hair," he agreed. Ruth Ann gave up in disgust. *He has absolutely no ideas*, she thought unhappily.

At the door he asked her, "May I see you again, Ruth Ann?"

"Sometime, Leonard," she managed to keep her voice pleasant. Leonard smiled and vanished, like the Cheshire cat, into the night.

The next Sunday morning Brian was beside her in Sunday school. Ruth Ann could feel his tall presence like a wound, but she would not let herself look at him. Mary hadn't been able to report on his whereabouts last Sunday night, but she was almost sure he'd taken Nelly out again. All right, if he preferred dazzling blonds with short hair, that was his business. Ruth Ann felt bitterness seeping into her heart and fought against it.

Brian leaned toward her. "May I come for you at seven tonight?"

Ruth Ann couldn't believe her ears. For a minute she said nothing. Fury and relief fought for expression. Relief won out as she whispered, "All right, Brian, I'll be ready."

Everything seemed as usual that evening. Ruth Ann

could almost have forgotten that anything had happened. They went to young people's meeting and drove home afterward. Ruth Ann waited for Brian to get out and open her door. When he didn't move, she looked at him questioningly. He was staring at her, his blue eyes dark and perplexed. "I know you're wondering about things," he said softly.

"Well, yes, a little," Ruth Ann admitted.

"Did you miss me?"

Fury stung Ruth Ann and she retorted angrily, "That is none of your business." She reached to open her door, but Brian slid toward her and caught her arm.

"Listen to me, Ruth Ann. Let me explain."

Ruth Ann felt his grip like a burn on her arm. "All right, but be quick about it. I haven't got all night." She wanted suddenly to hurt him and resisted an impulse to beat at him with her fists.

"How old are you, Ruth Ann?" The question caught her off guard. She stared at him in amazement.

"I'm sixteen. What has that to do with it?"

"Plenty. You're too young to go steady. I knew I shouldn't be monopolizing you the way I was, but I didn't know how to tell you. I found myself liking you too much."

Brian dropped her wrist and his arms were about her. "I missed you so much. Can't you see, Ruth Ann? This is what I was afraid of." Then he kissed her, and she felt the hard knot of pain in her heart evaporating.

She pushed him away, her eyes shining. "Why didn't you tell me this before? I wouldn't have minded hearing about Nelly Fisher so much if you had. I thought you were dating her because you couldn't stand my long hair anymore."

Brian frowned. "Ruth Ann, you know me better than that! I don't like people just because of the way they dress or wear their hair. You're special, Ruth Ann—very special." He squeezed her hand. Then he opened the car door. "Come on, Ruth Ann, we'd better go in."

As they walked to the house, he said, "Ruth Ann, I want you to be my special girl. You'll be free to date other guys, but remember, I'm coming back. OK?"

"Promise?" Ruth Ann asked soberly.

"I promise," Brian said.

# 10

## Christmas Cheer

Winter had come. Ruth Ann's boots swished through the feathery snow as she walked down the lane to meet the bus. She looked about her at the frosted fence posts and the whitening fields. Then she glanced at her watch. "Time to hurry, girls," she said to her sister. Donna lagged behind as usual.

"Hurry, cow tail," Terry called to her. "We're having our Christmas party today. You wouldn't want to miss that."

"We're having a party, too." Ruth Ann frowned. "I don't know what it will be like. I hope the kids don't decide to dance."

"Do you think they will?" Terry's eyes were wide with curiosity. "I'd like to see someone dance."

"It's not much to see," Ruth Ann assured her. "They dance in the gym during lunch hour sometimes. I looked in once or twice. It doesn't look like much fun to me."

"I don't care, I'd still like to see a real dance," Terry persisted.

"You exchanged names for your party, didn't you?" asked Donna.

"Yes, you saw the pair of socks I got for Tom Stanton," reminded Ruth Ann.

"Who has your name?" Jan asked.

"I haven't the faintest idea. Hurry now, girls, we'll miss the bus."

At school the desks were pushed to the sides of the room. Ruth Ann wished she had stayed at home. It was obvious a dance had been planned.

Roxy walked in smiling, "Cheer up, Ruth Ann," she said. "Christmas holidays are almost here."

Ruth Ann tried to smile, cheered by Roxy's kindness, but still wishing she were at home.

Then it was time to distribute the gifts. Ruth Ann held her package in her fingers, afraid to open it. Maybe someone would give her jewelry. The package was tiny. She read the card, "To Ruth Ann Miller from Scott Keeler." She looked about her. Oh, yes, that was the new boy. He'd been in school only a few weeks. Obviously the athletic type, he towered above the other boys. Ruth Ann didn't know him well, but she couldn't help admiring his clear gray eyes and the friendliness in his handsome face.

She pulled at the string about her gift. Slowly she unwrapped it and opened the little box inside. Roxy leaned over Ruth Ann's shoulder. "What did you get?"

Ruth Ann sat staring at a delicate little bracelet. "It's lovely," Roxy said, then seeing Ruth Ann's face, "but you can't wear jewelry, can you?"

"Sh," Ruth Ann said, seeing that Louella was listening. But Louella had already heard.

66

She snatched at the opportunity. "Who gave you that?"

"Scott," whispered Ruth Ann.

"Oh, boy! Scott, don't you know this little saint doesn't wear jewelry?" Louella rocked with laughter.

Some of the boys laughed. Ruth Ann didn't know who was laughing. Her eyes were still fixed on the bracelet. Scott must have meant this as a practical joke. Well, he had gotten his laugh. Ruth Ann got up, her cheeks burning, and rushed from the room. She stumbled to the washroom, her hands shaking with fury. Roxy and Cindy followed her.

"Don't take it so hard," Roxy pleaded. "Maybe Scott didn't know. He seems like a nice kind." But Ruth Ann couldn't stop shaking. "Maybe you'll feel better after Christmas," offered Roxy.

"Christmas! I wish I could stay home forever." Ruth Ann lifted angry eyes.

During the holiday, she tried to forget the bracelet, but it lay in a corner of her mind. The Christmas music which she loved so dearly failed to take away that little edge of displeasure.

On Christmas Day, Brian knocked at the door. "Hi." He offered her a package he'd obviously wrapped himself. It was a no-nonsense, no-ribbons kind of package. She looked at the card. "To Ruthie," she read. Brian sometimes called her that, and it gave her a tender, protected feeling. She wanted to fling herself into his arms and stay there forever, away from the uncertain world of school.

She opened the gift eagerly. "Oh, Brian, just what I needed!" Brian had chosen a pen set for her. The new pen wouldn't replace Drusilla, but it would certainly compete with her.

That evening Ruth Ann wrote in her journal, "If only all boys were as kind as Brian, this world would be a pretty good place. I hate to think of going back to school. I hope the kids have forgotten about the jewelry. I'm afraid I haven't." Ruth Ann capped Drusilla and sat admiring her new pen. She wondered whether it would like green ink. Drusilla seemed to thrive on it. She would have to think of a name for the new pen.

Then she sighed as she thought again of the bracelet. *Forget it, you foolish girl,* she told herself. But it was not easy to follow her own advice.

Back at school after the holidays, she walked along ignoring the students as much as she could. Once she turned her head and saw Scott Keeler following her. She walked faster. Then she heard a deep, masculine voice calling her. "Ruth Ann." She walked still faster. Scott fell into step with her. She pretended not to see him.

"Ruth Ann, please listen," he pleaded.

She stopped and saw that his eyes were serious. "All right," she said and stopped walking.

"Ruth Ann, I didn't know you couldn't wear jewelry," he said. "I never knew any Mennonites before. Can you blame me for not knowing that jewelry was forbidden? Won't you please let me make it up to you?" He took a neatly wrapped package from the paper sack he carried and handed it to her.

She held it for a moment, speechless. "Well, aren't you going to open it, Ruth Ann?"

"All right." She fumbled with the wrapping and uncovered a flat box. Should she open it, or was

Scott only trying to make a fool of her again? She slipped the lid off the box, holding her breath, then sighed in relief. The box held three lovely handkerchiefs. "They're beautiful," she breathed.

"I'm glad you like them," Scott said. "And I'm really sorry I upset you."

"That's all right." Ruth Ann smiled at him. "I'm too sensitive. It was really nothing, and you really are kind, Scott."

Scott laughed in relief, and they walked to homeroom together.

# 11
# Beautiful Beth

One day when Ruth Ann came home, a fat letter awaited her. "From Cousin Beth, I'll bet," she said. Cousin Beth could think of more things to write about!

She opened the letter with one slit of her thumbnail. "I've a chance to come to visit you," she read. "One of my older girl friends wants to visit your area, too. I already have my bus ticket. I'm anxious to see your school. Do you think I could go to school with you at least for one day? I know you dislike the school, but I'm curious about it anyway. I never saw a big secular high school. I'll be coming Wednesday. Reckon you could come meet me if I call when I get there?"

Ruth Ann folded the letter carefully and sighed. Cousin Beth at school! Oh, dear, what could be more awful? She loved Cousin Beth herself, but what would the kids at school think? Cousin Beth, who lived in the South, was an Amish girl. Since cars were forbidden by her church, Beth and her parents usually came to visit the Pennsylvania country only once a year. Then they traveled by train or bus.

A vivid picture of Beth was forming in Ruth Ann's mind. Her cousin wore her chestnut hair tightly drawn back from her face, and tucked severely beneath a prayer covering of thick black material. She was not allowed to wear skirts or blouses, but always wore a uniform type of clothing. Her dress was simple and long-skirted, covered by a half apron and a cape, a sort of second bodice. Ruth Ann often wondered why she didn't roast in the summer. Her legs, beneath her long skirts, were always clad in thick black stockings. With this picture of her cousin, Ruth Ann also saw in her mind the jeering boys at school. They would laugh and call out rude little remarks.

She thought briefly of writing Cousin Beth and telling her not to come. She wished she could think of some logical excuse. She pushed the problem from her mind. Maybe time would solve it. Cousin Beth was arriving on Wednesday, which was tomorrow. Maybe she would have so many other places to visit that she couldn't go with Ruth Ann to school.

The next evening when the phone rang at seven o'clock, Ruth Ann dashed to answer it. "That's Cousin Beth."

"I'm at the station," her cousin said. "Can someone come to meet me?"

"Sure, I'll get Daddy. We'll be there in a minute."

At the bus station the two girls spotted one another at the same moment. They rushed toward each other. "It's so good to see you." Ruth Ann hugged her cousin.

When they went outdoors, Beth put on her bonnet

71

against the chilly March wind. "I hate this thing," she mumbled under her breath. "Everywhere I go people stare at me."

Looking at her cousin, Ruth Ann could understand why people would stare at her. Her height set her apart. The strange stovelid type glasses gave an owlish look to her face. Her somber dress and severe hairstyle offset the bright glow of health in her cheeks. She had had firsthand experience with life in the country, milking eight cows by hand every morning. Perhaps this explained her mannish posture and the broadness of hip and back.

"Well, will you take me to school with you tomorrow?" Cousin Beth was never one to evade the issue.

"I don't know. I don't think you will like it. I told you how Louella and some of the boys act. Do you really want to go?"

"I sure do. I can take a little meanness. I've thought about this for months."

"All right, if you say so." Someone else had come to meet Beth's friend; so they started for home.

The next morning, as they dressed for school, Beth asked, "Are there any nice kids at school?" Ruth Ann had almost forgotten the delightful southern slur of Beth's voice.

"Oh, yes, there are quite a few, really." Ruth Ann didn't intend to give her cousin a false impression of the school.

On the bus Beth met some stares. *I'll bet they're thinking she looks like me, only worse,* thought Ruth Ann. *I shouldn't have brought her.*

She waited for the jeers that were certain to come. Joe Fisher always had fresh remarks. If he would

spend more time studying books and less time thinking of nasty things to say, the entire school would profit.

Joe did not fail her. As they entered the school, he came bouncing along. "Boy, wouldn't you like to go out with that good-looking girl?" he remarked loudly to his friend. Ruth Ann had a hard time keeping her tongue in her mouth.

"What's your name?" he asked.

"Beth Yoder."

"Oh, beautiful Beth," Joe laughed uproariously.

Joe trailed them all the way to homeroom, making appropriate remarks en route. Ruth Ann couldn't help glaring at him as he passed them. Sometimes she wished that she didn't have the reputation of her church to uphold.

*I'd like to be myself for just one day instead of being a Mennonite,* Ruth Ann thought in despair.

She looked at Beth, who winked at her and whispered as Joe passed, "I hope he's having fun!" How could she laugh when Joe was making fun of her?

The girls in homeroom were silent at first, trying not to stare at Ruth Ann's cousin. Then the questions began. Every girl wanted to know something about the Amish. "Why do you dress like that? Do you always live on farms? Why don't you like automobiles?" and on and on. Beth answered every question in thorough detail. Her calm expression did not vary. She answered the mocking questions with serenity.

In English class Beth did the assignment with the rest of the students. "I never finished high school," she explained to Mrs. Jensen. This led to a discussion of Amish beliefs about education. Before Ruth Ann realized what was happening, Beth had the floor,

74

explaining that Amish people don't feel higher education is necessary since they plan to work on farms all their lives anyway. "My dad thinks it is a waste of money," she said.

Ruth Ann sat with her head lowered in embarrassment. Why did people always have to know everything? She was tired of answering questions about her religion, tired of seeing people stare at Mennonites and Amish. Beth seemed not to mind answering questions, although she had said she hated the stares of people. Then she heard a new question.

"Do all these questions bother you?"

"Well, yes, sometimes." Beth grinned from ear to ear, brown eyes atwinkle, and it was almost possible to forget her strange attire. "Plenty of times I've wanted to stick my head in a hole, but I reckon this wouldn't work too well."

Ruth Ann looked at her cousin and felt a sudden pride welling up inside her. Beth looked far stranger than Ruth Ann had on her first day at the high school, but she was answering questions positively and keeping her sense of humor besides. Ruth Ann remembered her own reaction when someone had asked her whether she was going to the dance. Beth would probably have chuckled and said, "Can you imagine me dancing in this getup?" She had that rare ability of laughing at herself.

At lunch time while Beth was at the drinking fountain, Roxy said to Ruth Ann, "Your cousin is lots of fun. I wish she lived here so that we could get better acquainted."

"So do I," Ruth Ann said, and was surprised to realize that she really meant it.

# 12
# Whispers

Homeroom buzzed with activity that morning, but Roxy sat with lowered eyes. "What's wrong, Roxy?" Ruth Ann asked. But Roxy seemed not to hear. Tears etched lines down both her cheeks and her green eyes were unfocused and sad.

Ruth Ann sat down behind her friend. Roxy was usually so gay and lively; something must have happened to make her so dejected. Maybe someone else would know what Roxy's problem was.

In the hall after homeroom Louella was giggling with one of her friends. "Did you hear the news, Ruth Ann?" she asked in secretive tones.

"What news?" Ruth Ann turned puzzled eyes toward Louella.

"Oh, I thought everybody knew." The girl giggled again. Her shifty eyes darted from Ruth Ann to the door where Roxy was standing.

"Roxy's cousin has to get married," she whispered. She waited for Ruth Ann's reaction.

"Has to what?"

"Has to marry her boyfriend—you know—she's pregnant." Louella pronounced the word carefully.

"You mean Renee? I don't believe it." Ruth Ann longed to push Louella's suggestive eyes into her skull. "You're making that up," she said. Then as she looked at Roxy's sad face, she knew that Louella had told the horrible truth.

Her mind churned with thoughts as she walked to algebra class. Why hadn't she noticed the change in Renee? She hadn't heard anyone mention her pregnancy before. Of course, probably the other girls thought Mennonites would know nothing about such affairs or would not want to discuss them if they did know. Besides she was Roxy's friend and wouldn't have listened to any talk about her relatives. Ruth Ann shook her head to clear her mind. Renee. Beautiful, delicate, golden-haired Renee was going to have a baby.

When Ruth Ann had first seen Renee's lovely, sensitive face, she had thought of angels with pure white robes and harps of gold. Renee sang one morning during assembly, and Ruth Ann thought she could hear angel echoes. No wonder all the boys wanted to date her. Renee cared for no one but Jerry, a simple country boy with guileless eyes. They were always together. In the hall they walked with intertwined arms and dreams in their eyes. Ruth Ann had often envied Renee and wished Brian were not so stubborn in his insistence that she date other boys, too. She really didn't want to be with anyone but him. It would be so nice to feel that they belonged to each other. Some kids went steady at fourteen. She couldn't see why she and Brian shouldn't go steady.

Now Ruth Ann entered algebra class. Everyone was talking at once. "Did you know that Renee won't be graduating? She isn't in school today. The principal asked her not to come back." The voices hushed to a whisper as Roxy came into the room.

Midway through class Roxy nudged Ruth Ann. "Ask Mr. Bently whether you can go with me to the washroom." When Ruth Ann saw Roxy's drawn and colorless face, she moved quickly toward Mr. Bently's desk. "Mr. Bently may Roxy and I go to the washroom, please?"

Mr. Bently raised white eyebrows. "Two of you?" Then he saw Roxy's face and relented.

"Yes, you may. Perhaps the health room would be better."

In the hall Roxy said, "Ruth Ann, I didn't sleep at all last night. Mother just told me last evening about Renee. I suspected her pregnancy before, but I wouldn't let myself believe that it was true. Renee will soon be a mother." Roxy gripped Ruth Ann's arm. "I can't believe it."

Ruth Ann could find no words of comfort. She squeezed Roxy's palm silently. What could she say? There was no way of changing what had already happened.

That evening Brian came to take Ruth Ann to a Mennonite Youth Fellowship meeting. They hadn't been out together for several weeks. In the car Ruth Ann sat silent, unable to forget the events of the day.

"What's wrong, Ruth Ann—you aren't cross with me for not coming to see you sooner, are you?" Brian teased. "You were out with Leonard last week and wouldn't have had time for me anyway!"

"Oh, he's such a delightful person," Ruth Ann said, trying to sound sincere, but almost laughing.

"Oh sure," Brian said. "You really like him, don't you?"

Ruth Ann laughed. "You know I detest him. He's such a spineless fellow." Then she sobered. "I much prefer your company, Brian."

Brian looked at her from the corner of one blue eye. "Still want to go steady, Ruthie?"

Ruth Ann swallowed hard. Her heart cried out, *Yes, yes,* but aloud she said, "No, Brian. I think you're right in saying we shouldn't be too serious just yet."

Brian winked at her. "We have lots of days ahead," he said.

*Thanks to you,* thought Ruth Ann. But she could not help thinking of the miserable days in store for Renee.

# 13

# Sisters Are Human

Ruth Ann sat at the sewing machine, stitching a dress for her sister. There was no end to sewing in the Miller house. Janice, especially, managed to rip her dresses into shreds in an unbelievably short time.

Ruth Ann finished sewing together skirt and waist of Jan's dress and called for her sister. "Jan, come here. Try on this dress and see whether it fits you."

"Coming," Jan called from upstairs, where she was reading another book. Sometimes Ruth Ann envied her younger sisters. Her own carefree days were over, or had she ever had such days in her life?

"Here I am," Jan presented herself airily.

Ruth Ann held the dress up in front of Jan, measuring with her eyes. She frowned. "It looks a little small. I do hope I won't have to open it again."

"Don't start moaning before I even try it on," advised Janice. She pulled the dress over her head and began buttoning the front. She struggled with the last button and admitted, "It's a little tight."

80

"Oh, dear," Ruth Ann sighed in exasperation. "If only you weren't so fat, Jan."

Jan glared at her. "I am not fat, Ruth Ann. You can just keep quiet."

"Oh, all right," Ruth Ann mumbled with her mouth full of pins. "Forget it. I'll open this and see whether I can fix it." Wearily she went back to the task of fitting her stout sister. She would have to open the darts in the bodice and the seams of the skirt. She reflected that making a new dress would have been simpler.

Jan started taking off her dress. Ruth Ann heard the seams ripping. "Well, there's one seam I won't have to open." She looked at her chubby sister. *I hope someday you'll start losing some of that middle,* she thought.

This time Jan had no retort. She favored Ruth Ann with a frown and snatched the dress across her head. She flung the frock angrily at Ruth Ann and ran from the room.

*Oh, dear, I guess I shouldn't have said that. She doesn't like being plump any more than I like being thin.* Ruth Ann shook her head and began altering the dress. The incident soon left her mind as she became absorbed in work.

Later she looked out to see whether the wash was dry and saw Jan pummeling Terry with her fists. Terry leaped away agilely and started running up the road. Jan tore after her, her thick blond braids flapping.

"What's wrong, girls?" called Ruth Ann. Since Mamma was resting, Ruth Ann would have to serve as referee.

81

Donna, who was watching the quarrel, said with a grin, "Oh, Terry was teasing her about her front teeth. You know, they're shaped just like a ground-hog's!"

"Donna, how unkind," rebuked Ruth Ann and then fell silent as she remembered that only a moment before she had been no less unkind herself. *What makes us so cruel?* she wondered. *Why should we delight in another's suffering?*

That evening when the girls were doing supper dishes, the subject of marriage came up. "Jan, you'll never get married," teased Terry.

"And why not?" Jan was defiance itself with her snub nose uplifted and her gray eyes angry behind her glasses.

"Well, number one—you're too fat. Number two—your teeth are crooked. Number three—you've got freckles. Number four—your glasses make your eyes look blurry." With each number the fury in Jan's eyes grew. Ruth Ann thought for a moment that Jan was going to poke Terry then and there. Instead, she glared at Terry for a full minute, then turned and stamped out of the room.

"Well, Terry, you'll have to finish dishes yourself," Donna announced.

"Oh, no, I won't. You'll have to help, too."

"Nope." Donna started for the door.

"Just a minute, young lady," Ruth Ann said. "I have something to say, and I want both of you to hear it." The girls stared at her in surprise. The twinkle in Terry's long-lashed hazel eyes disappeared. Ruth Ann's scoldings were serious matters.

"I'm sure you girls know that Jan has been taking

a lot of teasing lately. I want both of you to put yourselves in her place, and think how you would feel if you were Jan. Finish your dishes, and then it's bed for both of you."

Both girls were silent as Ruth Ann gathered up her school books and started upstairs to do her homework.

As she neared the door of the room the four girls shared, she heard muffled sobbing. She stopped short —Jan! It wasn't like Jan to cry, but apparently she had reached the limit of her endurance. Ruth Ann stood there for a moment, wondering what to do. Mamma and Daddy had gone to the doctor. Once more she was in charge. Then she remembered her friend Mary. Armed with the knowledge of her friend's experiences she entered the room.

Dumping her books on the bed, she put an arm about her sister. "I'm sorry about everything, Jan," she said softly. For a moment she thought her sister would spurn her apologies. Then Jan flung herself into Ruth Ann's arms, sobbing angrily. "I know I'm ugly," she cried. "But why does everyone have to rub it in?"

"You aren't ugly, Jan," comforted Ruth Ann. "You are just going through what's called the 'awkward age.' Many girls go through this. You know Mary Hershberger, don't you?"

Jan sniffed and nodded.

"You probably don't remember how she looked when she was your age, do you?"

"I can't remember Mary Hershberger as being anything but divinely beautiful." Jan's voice held envious longing.

"Well, I hate to disappoint you, but that just isn't true. There was a time when Mary was definitely fat, not just plump, but fat. Her brothers never let her forget it for a moment either. I can remember Dick yelling after her, 'Elephant legs on a chicken.' You see, her legs were particularly fat."

"Well, what happened to her?"

"I guess we'll just have to say she grew out of it, and so will you. Jan, you have lovely gray eyes, and your nose will never be long like mine. When I was your age, I was all nose!"

Jan couldn't help giggling at Ruth Ann's nonsense. "You turned out pretty good," she said with a smile.

"Well, you will, too. And tomorrow we're going to work on one of those shift dresses for you. I'm sure you'll look nice in it." Ruth Ann squeezed Jan's hand and felt her sister return the pressure.

"Thanks, Sis," Jan said softly.

# 14
# Spring Fancies

Ruth Ann stepped out on the sun porch one evening. She could feel spring seeping into her pores. "Isn't it warm enough to camp in the cabin by now?" she asked Mamma.

"Yes, I think so. Why?" With the spring's return Mamma's pale cheeks had acquired a faint pink. She looked really alive again.

"I'd like to have some of my friends over some evening. Maybe we could sleep in the cabin. I'm sure they'd like that." Ruth Ann remembered the slumber party. She wanted to return Roxy's invitation.

"I believe we could manage it."

"I'll cook the supper," Ruth Ann offered, remembering that Mamma still spent a lot of time lying on the sofa. Aunt Etta did some of the laundry, but the housework and cooking were enough to tire one woman.

"That would help," Mamma said. "When would you like to invite them?"

"I'll check tonight. Maybe they can come tomorrow

night." Ruth Ann always liked to fit her words to action. Besides, the warm weather might not last long.

"All right. You go ahead with your plans, Ruthie. And let me know if I can help you." Mamma smiled, and Ruth Ann went to phone her friends.

For a long time Ruth Ann thought about Louella. Should she invite her? *Yes, I will,* she finally decided. *I'm not going to be petty.*

When phoned, Louella said coldly, "No, I'm busy tomorrow night." For a moment Ruth Ann felt hurt. She had really hoped Louella would get to like her. Then she thought, *Perhaps I imagined her coldness. Maybe she really is busy. I've got to be more like Beth.*

The other girls she phoned accepted immediately. She asked Roxy and Cindy first. Then Lila, Anna, and Retha all accepted.

Deciding what food to prepare, she boiled a large kettleful of potatoes. Daddy raised potatoes in the garden every summer and they had plenty. She could peel them for potato salad in the morning. Next she decided to attempt homemade baked beans. She put the beans in a large pan to soak overnight. She would have to get up early and cook them in the pressure cooker. Mamma would put them in the oven for her if she prepared the sauce. Then she mixed a huge meat loaf. While her eyes were still weepy from the onions she had used for the meat loaf, she mixed a cake and put it in the oven. She would have cake and some of Mamma's lovely golden-cheeked peaches for dessert.

Next day was blurry with plans and hurried preparations and all the excited gaiety at school.

That evening her girl friends all walked up the hill with Ruth Ann. "Do you have to walk every evening?" Cindy asked.

"Yes. It's not too bad unless you have lots of books."

"Ruth Ann studies too much," Donna remarked. "She should read to me more."

Roxy grinned at Donna and tweaked one of her fat braids. "What do you eat to make your hair so thick?" she teased.

"I like potatoes best. I want them for breakfast, dinner, and supper," Donna giggled.

As they reached the top of the hill, Ruth Ann suddenly thought about the shabbiness of the house. The woodsy gray of the shingles called out for paint. *Should I apologize for it?* she wondered. She decided, *No, they like me for myself, not my home.*

Ruth Ann's menu that evening was a success. The baked beans and salad disappeared in no time.

"Did you girls know you're going to sleep in the cabin?" Donna asked. "Mamma says I have to stay here and behave myself. I'd rather go along out and sleep with Ruthie. No one is as cuddly as she is."

"Nope, you'll have to sleep with Jan tonight. She doesn't like to be touched," explained Terry. "She gives me a shove if I dare to get on her side of the bed."

Jan glared at her sister. Ruth Ann decided the time had come to retreat to the cabin in the woods.

"You girls needn't worry about the dishes tonight," Mamma said. "The younger girls can help me with them."

Donna snorted, "That's the bad thing about having company—they never have to help with dishes."

"That will be enough, Donna." Mamma's look was enough to silence the little girl.

Outside, the woodsy freshness of springtime was everywhere. "This is heavenly," Roxy said.

All about them budding maples showed the first soft colors of spring. Robins caroled late notes and spring peepers seemed to be all over the valley.

They then came to the cabin. It was not really a cabin, but an old hen house that Daddy had done over for the girls after much urging on their part. He had been able to make bunk beds for them one winter when work was scarce.

"Boy, your dad must be swell to do all this for you," Cindy said.

"I'll say; this is neat," Lila added.

When they were fairly settled in the cabin, Cindy combed the snarls out of her long dark bob. "Why don't you take down your braids and let us comb your hair?" she suggested to Ruth Ann.

"Oh, all right. I don't mind." Ruth Ann took off her covering and pulled the pins out of her braids. Cindy opened the braids and gently combed the long hair.

"Have you ever cut your hair?" Roxy asked.

"No," Ruth Ann said.

"Might you sometime?" Cindy asked.

"I've thought about it. A few of the girls in our church have done it. My best boyfriend and I talked about it. Mamma and Daddy would have fits if I did; so I just think about it."

"I think you're pretty just as you are, but with

long dark hair swinging on your shoulders you would be even lovelier. Couldn't you cut it gradually? Then no one would notice at first," Cindy suggested.

"Some of the girls do this," Ruth Ann admitted. "But Mamma understands the Bible to say that if a woman cuts off any of her hair she is dishonoring her head. Some of our people say that Paul was speaking to the Corinthian women in particular and not with our society today in mind. Things have changed so much. Corinthian women with short hair were usually prostitutes. Mamma and Daddy can be pretty convincing." Her eyes grew wistful.

"I'd please myself if I were you," Cindy volunteered. "You can't please everyone."

"No, I guess not."

"Why don't you snip off only some of the ends?"

"Is there a pair of scissors here?" asked Cindy.

"Oh, yes, Donna keeps some out here for cutting out paper dolls." Ruth Ann opened the drawer and held the scissors in her hand. She flipped her hair back and forth. She sawed at the air with them. "I am tempted to do it," she said.

"Why don't you?" urged Cindy. "Think how pleased Brian might be."

Ruth Ann closed her eyes. "It would be nice not to be so different in school," she murmured.

"Do you mind it a lot?" asked Roxy.

"Sometimes I hate looking the way I do." It was good to voice the rebellion she must suppress at home.

"Well, why don't you cut off just a little for a start? I'll do it for you." Cindy grabbed the scissors and waved them. "Want me to?"

"Well, all right, but only a little." Ruth Ann felt her heart beat faster. She heard the click of the scissors behind her, then swiveled and stared at the dark heap of hair on the floor.

"I'm sorry, maybe I cut off too much." Cindy turned frightened eyes to Ruth Ann.

She still stared at her hair. With a few neat snips Cindy had cut off almost a foot of Ruth Ann's dark mass of hair.

"You'll never miss it. You've got so much left. You aren't mad at me, are you?" Cindy asked.

"No. I gave you permission to do it. It's just the strangeness of seeing my hair on the floor like that. It seems as though I'd lost a part of myself." She shook her head. "I can't explain it."

"I guess you won't be able to hide such a large loss of hair for long, will you?" Roxy asked.

"No, not with three sisters sleeping in my room." Ruth Ann had dreaded Donna's tattling tongue.

"I'm really sorry," Cindy apologized.

"Don't be. I'll do my hair in a bun. Then it won't be so obvious that it's been cut."

They dropped the subject, yet somehow the evening was ruined for all of them. The usual chatter and hilarity of slumber parties was sadly lacking. Ruth Ann lay in her bunk thinking.

*I shouldn't have done it*, she thought. *Mamma has had such a hard time. How will she feel when she finds out? Maybe I can persuade my sisters not to tell. Donna will tell. She can't help it. She was born with a wagging tongue.*

Had she done something truly wrong in cutting her hair? Ruth Ann wasn't sure. She finally fell asleep.

# 15
## New Horizons

The next day in study hall Ruth Ann brooded about her hair instead of doing her homework.

"Ruth Ann Miller, please come to the desk."

Her mind leaped from the thoughts about her hair to the present. She snapped shut her history book and walked to Mr. Bently's desk. What had she done wrong? Mr. Bently was known for his irritable disposition. Had she unwittingly made her desk screech? Ruth Ann still remembered the first day she had been in Mr. Bently's study hall. Sitting on the very front edge of her chair, she was absorbed in a book, when abruptly the chair deposited her on the floor with a crash. Mr. Bently scolded her roundly for carelessness and for disrupting the study hall. Then, too, she was sure he still remembered the cheating episode. At least she was doing well again in algebra since she had more time to study.

Ruth Ann's fingers twitched with impatience as she stood beside the desk. She wished Mr. Bently would get on with it. When she dared to look at the old gentleman, she was surprised to see a smile in his brown eyes. *He's really quite handsome with that silver hair when he smiles,* Ruth Ann thought in surprise.

"Mrs. Hammond would like to see you in Room 116. She's our journalism teacher. You may go now."

Ruth Ann gathered her books and started down the hall to Mrs. Hammond's room. What could Mrs. Hammond want with her? Ruth Ann had often seen her. A tiny birdlike creature, she seemed to flit up and down the hall.

Ruth Ann paused at the door of 116. She hoped she looked less frightened than she felt.

Mrs. Hammond looked up from the untidy clutter of her desk. "Oh, there you are, Ruth Ann. Please come in."

Ruth Ann walked in shyly, glad for the books to occupy her hands. She noticed that the room was empty of students. Mrs. Hammond apparently wanted to see her alone.

"Sit down, Ruth Ann. I'd like to talk to you for a few moments." Mrs. Hammond's hand fluttered about, jingling the bright necklace around her throat. Ruth Ann glimpsed faint streaks of gray in her neatly waved hair. She would be about Mamma's age, Ruth Ann guessed.

Putting her books on a desk, Ruth Ann sat down. Apprehension still clouded her mind. Why didn't Mrs. Hammond tell her what she wanted?

"I understand that you write, Ruth Ann." Mrs. Hammond's voice was light and birdlike, too. Relief washed the anxiety from Ruth Ann's face as she realized what the little woman had said. Mrs.

Hammond wanted to talk to her about writing.

"Oh, yes, I love to write." Ruth Ann propped her elbows on the desk beside her books, her dark eyes alight with interest.

"Yes, Mrs. Jensen has told me about some of your work in English class. She especially mentioned one story that she thought was excellent. I'd be very much interested in seeing some of your work, Ruth Ann. My husband is a publisher, and I'm always interested in students who have writing ability. Would you like to bring me some of your work sometime?"

"I'd like that very much." Ruth Ann was breathless with surprise.

"You might bring it to me tomorrow during your study hall. I'll give you a pass to Mr. Bently. I'm anxious to see your work." Mrs. Hammond smiled in dismissal, and Ruth Ann moved lightly from the room. *Mrs. Hammond wanted to see her work!* She felt giddy with anticipation.

Quickly she began to plan what she would take. Mrs. Hammond had mentioned the story Mrs. Jensen liked. She would borrow Aunt Etta's typewriter and retype that. She might take a few of her best poems.

The next morning she was careful to get up before her sisters did. She rolled her hair quickly into a bun as she watched her sisters from the corner of her eye. *Don't wake, please,* she thought apprehensively. But they slept on until the alarm clock rang at seven.

That day Ruth Ann thought study hall would never come. She longed, yet dreaded, to hear what Mrs. Hammond would say about her work. Perhaps she wouldn't like it—how embarrassed they would both be!

94

When Ruth Ann finally found herself outside Room 116, she heartily wished she had stayed home. She clutched her books tightly and opened the door. Mrs. Hammond, grading a stack of papers, looked up when Ruth Ann entered. "Oh, dear, these papers," she groaned. "They are so elementary!"

Ruth Ann handed her little booklet, containing a story and several poems, to Mrs. Hammond. She had worked late into the night, trying to make them as attractive as possible. She sat down, both eager and fearful. Would Mrs. Hammond glance over her work and label it silly and elementary?

For a moment Ruth Ann stared at her notebook, afraid to watch Mrs. Hammond's face. She had given her the story she'd written about her first day at school. Using fictitious names, she had woven a story about her fright and then her acceptance of a new life.

When Ruth Ann dared to look at Mrs. Hammond's face, she saw her wiping away—was it tears? Mrs. Hammond caught her gaze and smiled. "This is touching, Ruth Ann. You must have felt this story very deeply."

Ruth Ann nodded, speechless. Mrs. Hammond was admitting that her story had made her cry.

Mrs. Hammond folded the little booklet and tapped it lightly with her fingernails. "I feel that this is good, Ruth Ann. Did you hear the short story contest announcement this morning?"

"No, I didn't." She knew she had been thinking about her hair during morning announcements.

"I think you should enter the contest," Mrs. Hammond went on. "You have definite ability."

"Thank you." Ruth Ann's eyes shone. "I really

would like to enter the contest. What are the rules?"

"The rules are few." Mrs. Hammond smiled. "We put the contestants into a room cleared of books and reference material. One teacher stays with them to see that they don't copy. Contestants are given a certain amount of time to complete their stories. At the end of this time, contestants must give their stories to the judges. You'll have a week to dream up a plot. I really like your story, Dear." She smiled at Ruth Ann again.

Walking from the room, Ruth Ann's mind seethed with ideas for the contest story. She would think about her plot every day.

That evening she wrote in her journal, "Maybe I can forget my hair now. I have the story contest to think about. If I get up early enough, my sisters won't see me combing my hair. Oh, I wish I hadn't cut it! I gathered the sheared ends and stuffed them into a paper bag in my dresser drawer in the cabin. I wish I had  disposed of it somehow. I feel like a criminal. I should really go out and bury the bag in the ground. Donna often snoops in my things. I'm too tired to go now."

Ruth Ann looked at Donna's innocent face. *She wouldn't hurt me on purpose*, Ruth Ann thought. *I should do something about that hair, though.* She sighed and got into bed.

# 16

## The Wounded Eyes

Ruth Ann washed the supper dishes the next evening to settle a quarrel about turns between Terry and Donna. Mamma sat at the table mending Daddy's socks. Ruth Ann tried to keep her hair turned away from Mamma's view. Soon she would have to wash her hair; then the secret would be out, unless she could do it when Mamma was gone. Even then, hair as thick as hers did not dry in one hour.

"What's the matter with your hair?" Ruth Ann jumped guiltily at the sound of Mamma's voice. "It looks so oily. When did you last wash it?"

Ruth Ann suppressed a sigh of relief. Mamma had not noticed the shorter hair. "Yes, I guess I should wash my hair," she admitted. "It wouldn't dry tonight anymore, though."

"Where's Donna? She should be helping with the dishes."

"She probably went out to the woods. She was so mad at Terry, she was almost at the spitting stage. I guess she'll come back when it gets too dark." Ruth

Ann watched the foaming dishwater swirl down the drain and hung up the dishcloth.

She almost dropped the dishpan as the door banged open with Donna-type force. "Mamma," screeched the little girl, her pipestem legs flying across the kitchen. She catapulted into Mamma's lap. In dismay Ruth Ann saw the paper bag Donna carried.

"Look what I found! Someone's hair. It looks like Ruth Ann's." Donna turned the bag upside down. The scattered locks slithered across the table and stopped right underneath Mamma's nose. Donna must have been "paper dolling" in the cabin and looked in the wrong dresser drawer.

Ruth Ann watched in fascinated horror. This had to be a nightmare. Things like this just didn't happen. When she dared to look at Mamma, she thought of the eyes of the wounded deer she and her sisters had found last deer season. *Where have I failed? What have I done wrong?* the eyes seemed to mourn.

"I think Ruth Ann cut off her hair," Donna chattered. "Isn't that wicked, Mamma? You said we should never cut our hair, didn't you?"

Donna dashed to Ruth Ann's side and yanked at her hair. The blunt ends showed plainly when it tumbled about her shoulders. Donna stared at her and grinned her missing-toothed grin. "You look like a movie star, Ruthie. I like you that way."

Ruth Ann looked miserably at the floor. Why didn't Mamma say something? Anything would be better than this silence.

When she glanced up, Mamma had vanished into the bedroom. Ruth Ann thought she heard muffled sobs.

*Why didn't she scold me?* Ruth Ann thought. *That's much easier to take than her crying.*

"What's going on here?" Daddy came into the kitchen for his bedtime snack.

"Ruth Ann cut her hair." Donna pointed to her sister who was still standing in the middle of the kitchen. She pushed helplessly at the dark strands of hair.

"Ruth Ann Miller, how could you? You know better than that." When Daddy raised his voice, Ruth Ann always felt as though he still imagined her a small child. "Well, you've certainly spoiled your looks." Daddy's look of scorn pierced her heart.

Suddenly she could not keep silence. "That's what you think, Daddy. Donna thinks I look nice, don't you, Donna?" The child nodded and Ruth Ann's voice rushed on. "Brian will like it, too. Not everyone is as old-fashioned as you are." She ran from the kitchen and upstairs to her room. She grabbed a vase of flowers and flung them at the door. The splintering crash relieved her feelings. Donna came dashing into the room when she heard the noise.

"I'm sorry I brought the hair in," she panted. "I shouldn't have done it. I think Daddy's real mean. I'm willing to help you hate him."

Ruth Ann giggled hysterically at her sister's suggestion. "No, honey," she said. "I'm afraid that wouldn't solve anything. I suppose I've hurt Daddy's and Mamma's feelings. You know how you get sometimes when someone hurts you. You want to hurt them right back."

Donna nodded, her dark eyes glinting with understanding. "Well, I guess that's how Daddy felt. Then he said things that hurt me, and I wanted to hurt him back. It could go on and on."

Donna put on her pajamas and buttoned them. Terry and Janice came upstairs and started undressing. "We were playing badminton outside, and we heard an awful racket," Terry said.

"Sure sounded like a big fight," Jan added.

"It was." Donna liked being the bearer of bad tidings. "Ruth Ann cut her hair and Daddy and Mamma were pretty mad."

"Did you really?" Terry's eyes widened. "I wish I had enough spunk to do that."

"You'd better not," advised Ruth Ann. "Enough is enough. Mamma couldn't take any more right now. I shouldn't have done it. It's easy to blame other people, but the girls did egg me on the other evening."

After her sisters were asleep, Ruth Ann took out her journal and wrote, "The awful truth is out. I'm relieved in a way. I couldn't expect to hide it anyway. I guess things will be rough for a while. Mamma won't be speaking to me without tears in her eyes and Daddy will glare for several days. I'm not ready to say I'm sorry either. I guess I'm stubborn, but for once I wanted to do things my way."

Ruth Ann slid her journal under the mattress and turned off the light.

She looked with aching eyes into the blackness. *Where was God?* she wondered. Did He care about one small creature? He had so many people to look after. Did He really have time to listen to her prayers? Anyway, she didn't feel like praying. Hurt and anger festered side by side in her soul. No, she really couldn't pray. She moved about in the bed, searching for a more comfortable position. Then she remembered the short story contest and began planning her plot. She knew now what it would be—something about a girl in the kind of situation she herself faced.

"Write about what you know," Mrs. Jensen always said. Well, she would do it.

She lay there, her mind seething with ideas, but always she came back to Mamma's wounded eyes.

# 17
# The
# Contest

Ruth Ann's heart pounded faster as she stood in the hall outside Room 100.

The principal had announced that all persons interested in the short story contest should enter Room 100 at ten o'clock. Now she was here and wished she hadn't come. Maybe her story was trivial. Who would be interested in the feelings of a Mennonite girl? Maybe she should change her idea. But it was too late now; she couldn't think of a new idea before ten o'clock. Glancing at the hall clock she saw that it was nine-fifty-nine.

Mrs. Hammond opened the door. "Oh, Ruth Ann, I'm glad you decided to come. I'm sure you'll do a good piece of work."

She held the door as the students filed in one by one. Ruth Ann's heart sank as she watched the people who were entering the contest. Jim Sarger, the editor of the yearbook, Polly Fletcher, editor of the school newspaper, and most of the school's straight A students walked in and sat down.

A sense of finality hit Ruth Ann as Mrs. Hammond closed the door. It was too late for her to leave now. Her mind was still so filled with the anger and hurt of the past few days, she wasn't sure she could write anything.

Mrs. Hammond set her alarm clock and said, "When this rings in two hours, your time will be gone. You will hand your papers to me and I'll give them to the judges. The results of the contest will be announced in one week. You may begin now."

Ruth Ann lifted her pencil. How would she begin? She knew what she wanted to say, but the characters must carry the story, and she wasn't sure how the story would end.

Groping for the right beginning, she wrote a few sentences, crossed them out, and began again. She glanced at the alarm clock; she had already wasted ten precious minutes. Then the right character popped into her mind—a slim, dark-haired girl with eyes that could both flash in anger and soften with compassion.

Ruth Ann's pencil skimmed across the page. Her heroine rebelled against Mennonite ways, cut off her hair, and flung the trailing locks at her father's feet. She stamped in rebellion and screamed at her father that she hated him when he scolded her for what she had done. Her mother looked at her with tear-filled eyes.

Grim days passed for the heroine. Her father scarcely spoke to her, and her mother always wore a look of sadness. Finally the girl decided to make her peace with her parents.

She went to them and said, "Daddy and Mamma,

103

I'm sorry I did this against your wishes. I'll try to do better." The story ended with the family reunited.

Ruth Ann's eyes blazed with triumph. She had written her story and solved her problem at the same time. She had known all along that she was wrong in disobeying her parents' wishes. Anyway, she wasn't altogether convinced that it was right to cut off her hair. She needed more time to think.

She recopied her story and carried it up to Mrs. Hammond's desk just as the alarm rang. She didn't know whether her story was any good or not, but it had served its purpose. She knew what to do next.

Mrs. Hammond smiled at her. "We'll be eager to hear the results of the contest."

"Oh, yes, and I wonder who'll win," Ruth Ann said, watching all the brilliant students who had entered the contest.

"I don't know," Mrs. Hammond said, "but I have a feeling you'll be somewhere at the top."

"Thank you, Mrs. Hammond, but I'm not at all sure."

That evening on the bus Ruth Ann laced her fingers together tightly as she thought of what awaited her at home.

As she and her sisters got off the bus and started up the hill, Donna said, "Boy, I sure hope Mamma won't look sad this evening again. Daddy hardly smiles at all anymore. We don't have any fun since you cut your hair, Ruthie."

Ruth Ann frowned thoughtfully. "You're right," she said. "Maybe it will make you feel better to know that I plan to apologize this evening."

"Will you really?" Jan looked up in surprise. She

knew how hard it was for Ruth Ann to admit that she was wrong. "You mean you're really sorry that you cut off your hair?"

"Yes, I guess you could put it that way."

"Do you think it's wrong to cut your hair?" Terry demanded.

"I'm afraid so because of the way we believe about it." Ruth Ann thought deeply for a moment. How much should she say to her young sisters? They looked up to her, she knew. "Maybe someday I'll figure things out," she said. "Right now, I know one thing. It's wrong to disobey your parents and make the whole family unhappy."

"I guess you're right," Jan agreed.

As they neared the house, Ruth Ann felt her mouth grow dry with misgiving. Would she be able to carry out her intentions? Then she saw Daddy and Mamma in the garden. They were having a serious conversation.

Ruth Ann started toward them. Her three sisters trailed after her. They wanted to hear every word.

# 18
# The Winner

Ruth Ann was trying to think of a way to begin her apology when Daddy looked up.

"Oh, there you are, Ruth Ann." His face was stern and unsmiling. "Mamma and I have just been talking about you. We've decided that you shouldn't see Brian anymore."

Ruth Ann's heart almost stopped beating. Not see Brian anymore? This was unthinkable.

"Why not?" she cried indignantly.

"Didn't he influence you to cut your hair?" Daddy asked.

Ruth Ann said, "No."

"Well, then, who did?"

"But—" Ruth Ann began.

"No buts," Daddy's voice was grim. "I don't want you to see Brian again and that is that."

Ruth Ann turned and ran to the house. What use was there in saying she was sorry now?

*I'm not sorry*, she thought, *not now*. She rushed upstairs to her room. She pulled *Dramatic Events* from beneath the mattress and began to scribble angrily. "I hate him, hate him, hate him," she wrote, stabbing the paper with Drusilla's point. "He spoils everything for me. I can't forgive him for this. If I thought I could get away with it, I'd go out with Brian anyway. But Daddy would find out, and then where would I be? What will I say when Brian calls next time? He doesn't even know that I cut my hair. I won't know what to say to him. Oh, Daddy, Daddy, how could you be so cruel?"

Ruth Ann would have liked to write to Beth about her problem, but she wasn't sure Beth would be on her side. Beth wanted to dispose of her bonnet, but Ruth Ann doubted that she had ever seriously questioned the Amish position on long hair. She wanted to talk to her sisters, but they might tell Daddy. She would have to rely on her journal for comfort. Feeling alone and unloved, she rested her aching head on the bed.

The next days were full of heartache. "I thought you were going to tell Daddy you were sorry," reminded Donna.

"Not anymore, I'm not. He spoiled that for me." Ruth Ann's young face hardened.

"Well, I wish families wouldn't fight," Donna said. "I don't know whose side to be on. If I take up for Daddy, you'll be mad at me, Ruthie. If I take up for you, I can't sit on Daddy's lap."

"Don't worry about it, Dear." Sudden pity for her little sister made Ruth Ann reach out and hug her. "Maybe things will be better soon." In her heart she didn't believe it, but she hated to see Donna looking so unhappy.

The week passed slowly. Meals were unhappy, with little conversation. Ruth Ann tried not to look at Mamma's eyes. Sometimes she had a feeling Mamma wanted to say something to her, but couldn't.

Ruth Ann was glad to escape to school. One morning Roxy said to her, "Did you know that the winners of the short story contest will be announced today?"

"No," Ruth Ann's face brightened with sudden interest. "Oh, well, Polly Fletcher will probably win the prize. I might as well not listen."

"She—" said Roxy as the PA system started buzzing.

"Your attention, please," the principal said. The room quieted. "We are announcing the winners of the short story contest," he went on. "Third prize was taken by Polly Fletcher. Second prize goes to Jim Sarger." Ruth Ann blinked in surprise. The voice paused dramatically, then went on, "First prize goes to Ruth Ann Miller for her story, 'The Odd One.' "

The rest of the announcement was lost in the hum that followed. Roxy and Cindy were both trying to hug Ruth Ann at once. "I can't believe it, I can't believe it," Ruth Ann kept repeating.

When her sisters got on the bus that evening, Ruth Ann bubbled over with the news, "Girls, guess what? I won the story contest." Her sisters listened with shining eyes.

"I can hardly wait to tell Daddy," Donna said.

"Daddy?" Ruth Ann had forgotten all about Daddy for a few hours. "Maybe we shouldn't tell him," she suggested. Daddy would want to see the story she had written, and she wasn't sure that would be a good idea.

108

"Oh, but you've got to tell him," Terry urged. "If you don't tell him, I will," she added.

"Oh, all right," Ruth Ann relented.

The girls hurried up the hill together. "I can hardly wait," chattered Donna.

"This is really exciting," Jan said.

Her sisters ran ahead of Ruth Ann to tell the news. When Ruth Ann got to the house, Mamma was there to hug her. "I'm so happy for you," she said.

Daddy stood at the door, his eyes proud. "Did you really win first prize, Ruth Ann? Let me see the story you wrote."

"Oh, it's nothing, really," Ruth Ann objected. "I don't think you'd enjoy it."

"But I want to see it," Daddy insisted.

"Oh, all right." Daddy wouldn't give her any peace till he'd seen the story; so Ruth Ann reached into her notebook for the first copy she had written during the contest and kept in her notebook since.

She stood silent while her father's eyes moved rapidly over the smudged pages. Would he be angry?

When he reached the last page, he looked up and read aloud, "I'm sorry I did this against your wishes. I'll try to do better." He stopped reading and looked at Ruth Ann for a long moment.

"I guess it's my turn to say I'm sorry, Ruthie," he said. "You were going to apologize to me and I spoiled the whole thing. Let's forget about your hair for the time being and all be friends again."

Donna danced about them singing, "Oh, Happy Day," while her sisters all smiled. Even Mamma's eyes were bright once more.

"Can Ruth Ann date Brian after all?" Terry asked.

"I think maybe that would be all right. That is, if he asks her out." Everyone joined Daddy's laughter.

The next evening Brian called her. "Want to go for a drive?" he asked.

"Sure," Ruth Ann agreed.

She was waiting for him when he arrived. "Where are we going?" she asked.

"Oh, maybe past the high school and out to the lake."

"I'd like that," Ruth Ann said. "Could we stop for a minute at the school? I just feel like looking at it."

"You mean you don't spend enough time there?" teased Brian.

"Well, school will be over before long," she said.

"All right, I'll stop if you'd really like to."

At the school they got out of the car. Ruth Ann looked at the building, thinking of the past year. She had met so many new situations this year, and they centered about the school. She had struggled there with algebra while Mamma lay near death in a hospital. The true meaning of honesty had come to her after she copied from Cindy's paper. She had learned that she really had some writing ability. She had less hair than she had at the beginning of the year. She touched the bun at the base of her neck. It would grow out again. She caught Brian staring at her.

"What's wrong?" she asked.

"It's your hair," he said. "It looks different. You didn't cut it, did you?"

"Yes," she admitted. "It's been cut."

Then she told Brian about the cabin experience. She told him also about winning the prize story contest and how her father read the story and how it

110

brought happiness back into their family life again.

Brian was silent for a while and Ruth Ann waited for him to speak. Finally he looked at her and she imagined she saw a bit of mistiness in his eyes.

"I'm sorry you've had so much trouble. But you know it's you that I care for and not your hair. You have always been so neat in the way you put up your hair. It always made you look so attractive," he said quietly. He took both her hands in his and she knew by the look in his eyes that he really cared for her.

Ruth Ann smiled. Brian was the best thing that had happened to her this year. Many tomorrows waited for her, and she would go on making discoveries in the outside world.

*The End*

www.ingramcontent.com/pod-product-compliance
Lightning Source LLC
Chambersburg PA
CBHW071105260626
47162CB00006B/2211